Elisha Winfield Green

Life of the Reverend Elisha W. Green

One of the Founders of the Kentucky Normal and Theological Institute

Elisha Winfield Green

Life of the Reverend Elisha W. Green
One of the Founders of the Kentucky Normal and Theological Institute

ISBN/EAN: 9783337416201

Printed in Europe, USA, Canada, Australia, Japan

Cover: Foto ©Raphael Reischuk / pixelio.de

More available books at **www.hansebooks.com**

LIFE

OF THE

REV. ELISHA W. GREEN,

ONE OF THE FOUNDERS OF

THE KENTUCKY NORMAL AND THEOLOGICAL INSTITUTE—NOW THE STATE
UNIVERSITY AT LOUISVILLE; ELEVEN YEARS MODERATOR OF THE
MT. ZION BAPTIST ASSOCIATION; FIVE YEARS MODERA-
TOR OF THE CONSOLIDATED BAPTIST EDUCA-
TIONAL ASSOCIATION

AND OVER THIRTY YEARS PASTOR OF THE COLORED BAPTIST
CHURCHES OF MAYSVILLE AND PARIS.

WRITTEN BY HIMSELF.

MAYSVILLE, KY.
THE REPUBLICAN PRINTING OFFICE,
1888.

PREFACE.

For some time I have considered prayerfully the matter of writing a sketch of my past days; but not so much of the present, for it speaks for itself. When I am dead some profound, scholarly and energetic historian can portray my present days to the ages yet not born. I have only endeavored, as far as I could remember, to tell the most interesting incidents of my life as a slave and my life as a minister of Jesus Christ. If in this I have failed, then I apologize to those under whose eyes these lines may chance to fall. I am by no means a learned man, neither a historian nor a scholar. What little I know was the result of the opportunities of a slave. I secured Brother Butler's service to write while I dictated. Brother Butler is responsible for many utterances of elegant diction of speech. His services have been of much value. Many of my associate ministers have gone down to the grave. Adams, Lee, Monroe, Braxton, Clarke are now sleeping the sleep of the dead, and yet Dupee and Campbell and myself survive them. But our days are passing away and it may be soon that we shall rest with them. By the grace of God, if I live in the future as I have in the past, I can, when I come to die, say like Paul: "I have fought a good fight, I have finished my course, I have kept the faith." I ask God's blessings upon this volume wherever it may chance to fall. E. W. GREEN.

Maysville, Ky., 1887.

BISHOP DUPEE'S LETTER.

Dedicated to Bishop E. W. Green, of Maysville, Ky.

October 18, 1886.

In 1851 I made the personal acquaintance of Elder Elisha Winfield Green, then pastor of the Second Baptist Church of Maysville. We met in Lexington, where a most intimate and loving acquaintance was formed, and it has ripened into that brotherly love that Paul speaks of in Hebrews xiii-1. Brother Green is a Baptist of Bible type, and a Christian gentleman of the highest order—an able and successful minister of the New Testament. He has been pastor of the church of Maysville ever since the year 1844, and has devoted his time to that and to the High-street Baptist Church of Paris ever since the year 1865, and has supplied both of the churches as pastor with satisfaction and success. Truly astonishing, for he has preached in the following named places in protracted meetings: For the Rev. London Farrel, of Lexington; Elder Henry Adams, of Louisville; Elder James Monroe, of Frankfort; Elder Wallace Shelton, of Cincinnati, and he has preached in Paducah for the writer, and many and very many other places, and in all he has been successful and the Lord has-blessed his labors abundantly.

He was a distinguished minister in the State Baptist Convention and General Association, and filled an important office in both. For a number of years he was Moderator of the Mount Zion Baptist Association and he is now Treasurer of the Consolidated Educational Baptist Association.

Brother Green's value to his people as a Christian gentleman, as an efficient minister of the gospel and a successful pastor, and as an intelligent and useful citizen, cannot easily be estimated. He has few enemies, but like Paul, they hate him without a cause. He is a faithful and fearless expounder of the Word of God—a minister and advocate of the doctrine of one Lord, one faith, one baptism, and of the doctrine of the final perseverance of the saints.

Now, in regard to his marriages, he was exceedingly lucky in his first marriage with Miss Susan Young, for she certainly was an exceptionally good Christian lady and wife, with whom the Bishop spent all the days of her marriage relation with that degree of happiness characteristic of Abraham of old. And he says he has begun a repetition of the same kind of blessing and happy life in his second marriage.

Now I pray that God may keep and preserve him and bring him after labor to reward is the earnest prayer of his friend and co-laborer in Jesus Christ. GEORGE DUPEE,
Washington-street Baptist Church, Paducah, Ky.

TRIBUTE OF A FRIEND.

Maysville, Ky., December 2, 1887.

Rev. E. W. Green, Pastor First Colored Baptist Church: Having learned of your autobiography and history of the church, I think it my duty as a friend of almost half a century to say a few words. I have known the Reverend Mr. Green since I was a boy, when I came to Maysville to go into business in the wholesale house of John P. Dobyns. He was an employe in the house, like myself, for many years. I had the opportunity of studying him perfectly. He was always kind and courteous, faithful and honest, and a true Christian. He prepared himself for the ministry during the time and organized his church and built his house of worship—which has been since torn down and rebuilt—and he now has one of the largest and handsomest churches in the city. His works have been of more benefit to his race than everything else combined. May he live many years to continue his good work and when he leaves his present home may it be to enter a far better and more glorious one above, and receive the crown of eternal life at the right hand of God, is the prayer of his old friend,

JOHN M. STOCKTON.

CHAPTER I.

I WAS born in Bourbon County, near Paris, Ky., six miles to the right of that place, on the Georgetown turnpike. The date of my birth I am not prepared to mention, because the book that had the ages in it was burned. I lived in Bourbon County until I was ten years old; then I came to Mason County, where I now reside. Some instances which took place in Bourbon while I was there I have forgotten, and a few I remember yet. For instance, the following: The name of the man I lived with in Bourbon was Judge Brown. My mother, sisters Charlotte and Harriet and the balance of the children were then divided among the heirs of Dobbyns—sister Evaline to Silas Devaugh; brother Marshall to the same man; brother Alvin to Thomas Perry; brother Henry to Thomas Dobbyns; brother Elijah to Enoch Pepper. I might say here, so far as to the incidents of slavery and the other acts of this time, I have no knowledge to present in this sketch that in my estimation would be of interest to any one.

In 1828, as near as I can remember, I went to Mayslick, Ky., a small town distant about twelve miles from Maysville, in the same county. Mayslick is one among the oldest towns in the State. I think it has been noted for a Baptist Church since the year 1792. I went to that place and lived with J. L. Kirk, who married my young mistress, Jane P. Dobbyns. While with him, of course, as usual where slavery existed, I saw very rough times. While there I cooked, washed, spun flax and yarn, and did all the house-work the same as a woman. Here was where a man became a woman if such ever were possible in the history of the world. I lived here about four years—from 1828 to 1832. When Mr. Dobbyns had been dead awhile, my old mistress married Mr. Walter Warder. My sister and four children and myself were sold in Washington, Mason County, Ky., at a sheriff's sale. When we were put up to be sold, Mr. Oliver Kale refused to "cry" us off, and a man by the name of Charlie Ward supplied the place. After the selling, we then broke up at our old home and my mistress rented a place on the Lexington turnpike, where she remained three or four years. She then married the Rev. Walter Warder, as I have stated elsewhere. This act of selling colored people was considered by many as being of a low character, while there were those who thought it right, and to sell a negro was nothing more than selling a mule. After my mistress had married Mr. Warder, we then moved near the North Fork, on a farm that formerly belonged to Benjamin Fitzgerald. I remained with Mr. Warder some time, until his death.

I will mention an instance which occurred before I left Bourbon. It should have been mentioned before this, but I happen to think of it since. I well remember that at one time before leaving Bourbon County I attempted to attend Sabbath school—well, in fact, I did attend a kind of Sabbath school, gotten up by some of the blacks on the place and in different portions of the neighborhood. I, with some others, went and about the time we had gotten in a good way enjoying ourselves, the Patrollers came and whipped all of the grown persons in the schoolhouse. But, being very small, when they came in I ran out, passing under the arms of one that was standing in the door. Having escaped I then had about a mile to go and I ran so terribly fast that when I reached home I was well nigh out of breath. I often look back at that time and now, whenever I pass that place, I draw the scene fresh in mind. About this time the colored people had meetings out in some place to themselves, and would prepare for the Patrollers. If it were near a road, they would go to each side of the road and stretch a grapevine across it about as high as a horse, so as to strike a man about his breast. Those in the house would come out, sometimes with chunks of fire to make the men get from the door. The men, of course, not seeing the grapevine, would run into it and thus were thrown from their horses and the party would get clear. The object of the slaveholders was not to have the blacks gather in meetings or anything else, because, said they, when together that way, they (the negroes) would make plots to run off.

Another horrible crime I must mention here. About this time slave-traders would go to Virginia and buy up the negroes. Upon one Sabbath morning, I saw one with twenty-five or thirty colored men hand-cuffed and chained. There were three or four wagons within which were a host of women and children. Lawyer Payne, who was not then a member of any church and who owned slaves himself, said that a colored person should never again be brought through the city in that fix on Sabbath morning. And on another occasion I saw in Mayslick another company of forty or fifty men, chained in the same manner as those mentioned before. There were some five or six wagons loaded with women and children. The foremost man looked to be about seventy years old, and he was singing: " Hark from the tomb." Mrs. Ann Anderson, a white woman who was sitting at the window, could not help crying. Indeed it was enough to have moved a heart of stone. It would, in my estimation, have moved the feelings of the most treacherous man or woman in the cause of slavery. It was a scene upon which I looked with horror, the objects of the scene being my brethren, according to divine creation, the same blood running in their veins as in mine, and, being under the same yoke of bondage, I felt for them deeply in my soul. But I was unable to assist them in the least. I cannot picture the scene as it of right deserves, because my language is such that it will not permit. But indeed the scene was horrible to behold. I believe that the stain of slavery and its degrading impressions will long linger in the minds of generations yet unborn.

I was converted on the farm of Mr. Walter Warder, about three miles to the left of Mayslick, Mason County. When converted I was plowing. It was one Friday morning, between 9 and 10 o'clock. Shortly after my conversion, I was taken down with scarlet fever. It was about six months after that I was baptized at Nicholas' Ford, on the North Fork of Licking river, by the Rev. Walter Warder.*

In 1835 I married Miss Susan Young. In 1838 I left my wife in the neighborhood of Mayslick as a servant of Mrs. Sissen and came to Maysville. They did not get along together very well, and Mrs. Sissen sold her, as she thought, to Mr. Peck, of Washington, Ky., who was trading in colored people, or rather slaves, because in those times we were not known as colored people. She sold my wife with the expectation of sending her south, or " down the river," as the expression was. My master, John P. Dobbyns, gave the negro-trader the money and sent him out there. He bought and brought her to Maysville and, being unable to keep her, he sold her and three children to John C. Reid. I do not know how long Mr. Reid kept them, but I suppose about ten years. My master bought her back again, leaving her in the hands of Reid, with the three children. She remained with John P. Dobbyns until he failed financially. Having made a final failure, they put her and the children up at the market for sale. For better information I will insert the following paper, which speaks itself:

*I once saw Mr. Warder baptize forty persons before breakfast.

To the Public:

Elder Elisha Green, the bearer hereof, is a minister in good and regular standing, of the Baptist Church, and an acceptable pastor of the African Church (Baptist) of the city of Maysville. By the pecuniary misfortune of the gentleman who owned his wife and children they were thrown upon the market for sale, and Elder Green was induced by the advice of many friends to become the purchaser of his wife and two children, at the price of $850. His means (although he and his wife labor faithfully and live economically) will not enable him to meet the payments as they become due, and he has been counselled to seek assistance to enable him to meet his payment. We commend him to the kind consideration of the Christian public, and particularly to the members of the Baptist Church.

Maysville, Ky., November 1, 1858.

> H. RAY,
> *Pastor of the Baptist Church, Maysville.*
> SAMUEL S. MINER,
> JOHN MCDANIEL,
> JOHN HUNT,
> A. M. JANUARY,
> THOMAS A. ROSS,
> ROBERT A. COCHRAN,
> JOHN SHACKLEFORD,
> SAMUEL C. PEARCE,
> MICHAEL RYAN,
> SAMUEL W. WOOD,
> JAMES A. JOHNSON,
> LEWIS COLLINS.

These thirteen men, whose names are signed to the paper, were very generous, shown from the fact that when I told them I could not purchase my wife and children, they drew the money from the bank and said it was for me, saying: "If you never pay it, we will never trouble your family." I worked and made the money and paid it back in calls in the bank. Mr. Collins, one of the gentlemen on the list, told me to come and take this house in which I am at present. He charged me $4 per month as the rent. He said that when I had paid him $300 in rent, he would give me a deed to the property. But for the fact that I was $850 in debt because of my family, I was a little cautious about doing so. When I had paid for my family, property had advanced several dollars. He had been offered $500 for the house that I was in. I then, in order to possess it myself, gave him $500 for the property. One lesson I learned from this, and that was that it will not pay to rent.

I had not been in Maysville long until I began a prayer meeting in the house of old sister Jennie Marshall, on Short street. A few brethren and sisters and myself continued to hold meetings in sister Marshall's house until the congregation became too large. We rented a house from Aunt Rosy Brannum. We stayed here till it became too small for the congregations. We then got a house for five years from Mr. Spalding, which house now stands by the side of the new church. I suppose you will be pleased to know how and by what movements I came to be a preacher, and also the incidents that pushed me forward to the occasion. I was sexton of the white Baptist Church for sixteen years, and while associated with them, seeing different displays and other movements in church, hearing various men preach, I, of course, was somewhat struck with the idea of doing something for God. I was not only sexton of the church, but a worshiper in there among the whites. They saw in me the gift to preach, and two or three of the deacons went to John P. Dobbyns, my master, and got the authority to license me. I knew nothing of it. This is the form of the license granted in those days to colored ministers, especially to myself:

At a regular meeting of the Maysville Baptist Church, May 10, 1845, the following resolution was unanimously adopted: Be it

Resolved, That Elisha Green, the property of John P. Dobbyns, of this city, has full liberty and permission from this day to exercise his gifts in the public before the colored population of this city or any others before whom in the providence of God he may be cast.

E. F. METCALF, *Church Clerk.*

Thomas G. Keen, who was then pastor here, met to ordain me, but I refused to be ordained. I was not ordained until about two years after this. Dr. Helm, Mr. Larue and Thomas G. Keen composed the council for ordination. On one Lord's day I was called to go up to the mouth of Cabin Creek to preach a funeral, and not knowing, Mr. Means, who is the undertaker now in Maysville, got a company and went up there for the purpose of protecting me. When I had gotten through preaching I came out of the door of the schoolhouse and my opponent walked around me and looked as though I was a lion. About this time one of my members moved to Ripley, O. I do not think she had been there long until she was taken sick and her sickness resulted in death. Whereupon, I was invited to attend her funeral. Upon receiving the invitation, I went down to the river with a pass. They refused to take me across on account of the "Fugitive Slave Law." Finding that I could not get across, I came back up town and got Mr. Thomas Matthews to stand responsible for my value should I have escaped, as they anticipated. Finally I got across the river. I said to the Captian of the ferry-boat:

"Were it not that I had a funeral to attend at Ripley I would go back home, because," continued I, "they are so afraid that I would run off. I have had a dozen chances to run off. I do not want freedom in that way."

In 1855 I went to Lexington, Ky., to assist Bishop George W. Dupee. When I had finished my service in Lexington, I went to Georgetown, about twelve miles from Lexington on the Cincinnati Southern Railroad. Bishop Dupee requested me to go and fill an appointment for him, as he was sick. When I arrived the church was crowded. I went into the pulpit, read a chapter, sang and prayed. I was in the act of taking my text when unexpectedly a white man came in with a stick in his hand. Having come about half way up the church, he knocked on the floor and asked if there were any white men there. The answer was "No." He then shook his stick at me and said:

"You come out of that pulpit, then."

Said I: "Very well," and I came out. I was stopping with Brother Vinson. Early the next morning Elder Larue, pastor of the white Baptist Church of Georgetown, who was also at my ordination, came to see me. He asked if I were in the house. Finding that I was there, said he: "Tell him that I want to see him." I came out according to request. He asked me when I was going home. I told him that I was going home to-day, for I was satisfied with Georgetown. When I said this to him, he replied to me, "You can stay here and preach as long as you wish."

I think I staid there and preached three nights after this. My work in Georgetown being finished for the present, I returned to Lexington from whence I had gone. Having an appointment to fill in Paris, I, in company with Bishop Dupee, went to the ticket office to obtain a ticket for Paris. I went to the office, called for a ticket, but failed to get it. The ticket agent said that he did not know me and therefore could sell me no ticket. He asked if there was any one near by that knew me and could be responsible to him for my purchasing a ticket. I told him that "Here is General Shafer, who lives in Maysville; he knows me." The ticket agent said that he did not know Shafer. Well, I got no ticket at last. Bishop Dupee told me to stand by the train till it started and then get on, "for," continued he, "you will get half way to Paris before the conductor gets to you, and should he put you off, you can walk the balance of the way."

When the train came up I got on, as I had been advised, without a ticket. Sure enough when the train got about half way to Paris, the conductor comes walking down the aisle very pleasingly. Holding out his hand, said he: "Give me your ticket." I told him that the ticket agent would give me none and therefore I had none. Upon this, he inquired where I was going. I told him "to Paris." In order to cut off the conversation, I asked him what the price was. He told me that it was eighty-five cents and passed on. I never saw him any more till about two years afterward, when going to Lexington again. He was sitting in the same car, not far from me. I told him that I had been wanting to see him since 1855. Looking much surprised, said he, "What for?" I told him according to law he should have put me off the train, and then asked his reasons why he did not. He told me that my face satisfied him. I told him: "When I was on your train that day I thought you would watch me to see whether I got off at Paris." He said that he never thought of me any more.

CHAPTER II.

THE "Underground Railroad" deserves to be mentioned here. The President of this movement, Mr. Carbin, lived in Avondale, O. I went there to dedicate a church. While preaching, I discovered in the congregation an old lady sitting in the middle portion of the church with an old fashioned Methodist bonnet on. At the time I never knew who the woman was, but took good notice of her bonnet. The next day being Monday, I thought before leaving to visit my niece. In passing Mr. Carbin's house, he asked if I were the preacher. I replied that I was. He invited me in. I accepted the invitation and went in. When I was seated, he called his wife, who was in another room. He told me that his wife was out yesterday and heard me preach. I replied that I noticed during my preaching a lady sitting in the church with an old fashioned bonnet on. Said he, "Yes, that was she." He said that he had been the President of the "Underground Railroad" for a number of years, and began telling a joke on his wife. He said: "I must tell you a joke on my wife. There was a family that came from the south up here to spend the summer. They had with them a very nice young colored lady who did not wish to go south any more. I studied and could not fix any plan to get her from slavery without creating a disturbance," and that he did not want to do. So finally he told his wife about it. She said that she could fix a plan to get her. He said that his wife saw the girl and posted her that upon a certain day when the whites had sat down to dinner for her to leave and come to our house. The girl did so, and upon the first opportunity she came over. His wife got a common sized pillow, made a fine dress and dressed the pillow; put a bonnet over it as a head for it, secured a vail for the girl, one for the baby. She dressed very fine and started the girl before her, having the pillow as a baby. They went to the starting point, put the girl on and tore the baby up, came back nome, took the vail from her face. They never did know who it was. Thus the girl escaped from slavery into a land of freedom.

This "Underground Railroad" was not, as some thought, a railroad under the ground, but only assistance rendered a slave to obtain his freedom, or to escape from slavery to the land of freedom.

When I came to Maysville in February of 1838, I was hired to Leach & Dobbyns. While here sometimes I would be called upon to weigh salt and sugar, and in this way I learned the figures. I would weigh hemp and many articles about the house. As I thought that I had been called to preach I desired to read the word of God. I spent all the time that I could spare from my work at night and the time I had during the day at reading. I kept my book in the third story. In the summer season, when work was slack, I would go up there endeavoring to study and read the Bible.*

Being frequently called from my studies, they not knowing what I was doing, my boss would say to me, "What in the h—l are you doing up there?" Well, I went on after this for some years, having been much benefited.

I commenced preaching in Flemingsburg (a small village about six miles from Johnson's Station) in 1853. I was compelled to preach wherever I could get a chance. While at Flemingsburg, there being quite an extensive movement to get a colored Baptist Church. I went into the Methodist Church and preached in there, having been granted the use of their house of worship. While preaching in this church I did very well for some time until they (the Methodists) saw that the influence of the Baptists, through my instrumentality, was becoming strong. They contracted that I should preach in the church on a certain Sunday, as I was obliged to be at home at night. Frequently they would hold class-meeting till 12 o'clock, and therefore this cut off my preaching in the morning. As they had meeting in the evening again, Mr. Hendricks, the Presbyterian pastor, would frequently let me have his church.

When it was so that I could not get this, I would be favored with the Christian Church. By this time the white Baptists saw that I was in the act of doing good, when they favored me with the use of their church regularly. I continued preaching here till 1855, at which time I was called to the church at Paris. When I left this place there were about thirty that had professed Christ under my administration. I

*The first Bible that I read through twice is on my table now. That has been forty years ago.

frequently preached in Bracken, Lewis and Fleming Counties.

The next thing was to witness the selling of my son John. After Dobbyns' misfortune, he kept John for his own use, and failed to pay for him. Therefore he was sold to Roe Pearce. Pearce in turn sold him south. As it happened, my wife and I were going to Paris and when we got to the "Blue Lick Hills," in the month of December, we met our son John. He was tied, being in his shirt sleeves. Mr. Jack Hook,* who kept a livery stable in Paris some years and who is well-known there, was stage driver. Seeing him get on the stage in a tied condition, after riding about two miles, Mr. Hook urged them to untie him, saying that he would go his security. When we had eaten dinner at "The Lick," and started, he urged them that as John had on no coat to let him get inside of the stage. They did so and he rode from "The Lick" to Paris in the stage. When we got to the Paris jail, the stage stopped and our son John was put in jail. I then telegraphed to Mr. Pearce's father to keep him till I could get him a home. But instead of this they sold him to Wilby Scott, who took him south, and he was again sold in Memphis, Tenn., to a man that kept a livery stable. He staid with this man till the outbreak of the war. The man then sold out and went to Texas. All that I could hear was that war broke out in Texas, and many colored people were sent to Cuba. I heard nothing more of John. I suppose that he was in the crowd that was sold. The sight of this act I thought would break the heart of my wife. When the stage drove up to the steps, the proprietor came and opened the stage door. My wife was crying. He told her to hush. I said to him that that woman was my wife and that we had seen our son tied in ropes going south. Then said he: "Old lady get out." It was my son that I saw tied, sold and taken from me. Now as to the manner in which I considered the act. I considered it wicked and mean, not having the power to assist him in the least whatever. You can judge of my feelings at this time. But thank God that now there are no more such acts put upon our mothers, fathers, sons, daughters and wives. All my children were sold at a sheriff's sale except my daughter Amanda. The court had appraised my wife and four oldest children. And, according to law, they should have been put in jail. Mr. Watson Andrews went my security, I not knowing anything of the action. He went my security that my children would be forthcoming on the day of the sale. The court gave me the liberty of selecting them homes, which I did. And the nine gentlemen came together, and

*Mr. Hook was reared in Maysville and had played with my son John.

bought my wife and children at $850. They told me to go and make the money and pay it in "bank calls," but if I could not do this, none of them would trouble my family.

People may look at me now and say that I see an easy time and everything seems to be going well with me. If it is so, I can say that I have come through "floods and flames" to enjoy them. I have often been in a condition that I knew not what to do. It seemed sometimes that circumstances would overcome me, but I am thankful that Providence has always provided a way by which I could come out of those unhappy moments of discontent.

It pleased God to place my body under the influence of what is called inflammatory rheumatism. While I was sick, my young mistress, Alice Dobbyns, who was between eight and nine years old, would come up into my room to see me every evening when she had come home from school. One day she said to me: "Uncle Elisha, you must learn to write." I told her that I could not. Said she: "Yes you can, and I am going to set a copy for you." She began by setting me the alphabet, then set for me copies in writing. In a month I wrote a letter to my brother, who was at that time in the State of Missouri. Finding that she had given me much information about writing, I asked my master if I could make her a present. He said that he had no objections. I bought for her a ten-dollar gold pencil.

Afterward, when I would be on my way to Paris, meeting with "negro traders," they would inquire of me where I was going. I would tell them that I was going to Paris to preach. They would then ask me if I could write. I would tell them that I could. Then, not satisfied, they would ask who learnt me. I would tell them my young mistress, John P. Dobbyns' daughter.

I began preaching in Paris, July, 1855. And to begin my ministry at this place was no small task. Indeed, it was, of course, in the midst of that foulest of crimes, "brutal slavery." Many of the whites there thought me not capable of managing the ordinances and other pastoral duties of the church more than to preach. I would not submit to their opinions and said before I would be found so doing I would go home. or rather I would "get on the stage and go to Maysville." They seeing in my actions that I possessed some quality of manhood, and that if I could not rule I would not be ruled, yielded to my purpose. I think of this act as one the lowest ever committed under the sun. It was mean, treacherous, cowardly and unmanly in every form of perpetration. It was on the order of master and slave in the church of God.

When a few of the colored people of Paris, members of the white church, came out to be organized into a separate church, the pastor of the white church,* Rev. Mr. Link, drew up the following styled rules for the African Baptist Church:

I.   We adopt the same declaration of faith and practice with the Baptist Church of which we are members.

II.   We, as a church, will elect our own officers; call and maintain our own pastor; administer the ordinances to the church; receive, discipline, dismiss or exclude members only with the advice and approval of the church from which we are separated; *provided*, she will, at the proper time, by committee or otherwise, advise with us on any of these matters. If she does not, at our request, present to her pastor or deacons we will proceed in the fear of God to attend to these duties according to our own judgment.

III.   Our organization shall be styled "The First African Baptist Church in Paris."

IV.   We will elect delegates from the membership of the Baptist Church to bear our letter and represent us in the association to which said church belongs.

V.   We will report to the Baptist Church, or her clerk, as often as that church may direct, a strict account of our business and condition.

VI.   When we shall fail to comply with these obligations, or maintain properly the worship of God, or any other emergency shall make it necessary, the Baptist Church in Paris, by giving us two months notice and a hearing before them, if we ask it, may rescind the act of separation, and by so doing, all who are at the time members of the "First African Baptist Church in Paris," shall become members of said Baptist Church and subject to her discipline and care in all respects as we are now.

VII.   On motion it was voted that Elder Green, the pastor of the colored church referred to above, be authorized to receive members and attend to the discipline of the church in the absence of the white members of the church.

I would have you understand the distinction of the churches mentioned. "The Baptist Church," means the white church. "The African Baptist Church" referred to is the colored church. If you will read carefully the rules you will find that the colored church was a slave to the white Baptist Church. So long as we complied with their ideas and judgment in matters of worship, we could remain a separate and distinct church, but when we failed in their judgment to comply, the act must be rescinded and then all the members of the African church were back in the white church. It was not even in our power

*The white Baptist Church sat, at that time, on the Winchester pike, on the left-hand side of the railroad going to Lexington from Paris, a little this side from Mr. Thomas' planing mills.

to select delegates from our church; this the whites did. After the organization, the City Council held a meeting in which it was proposed to limit our meetings to 9 o'clock—that is, night meetings. Major Williams told the Council that proposition would not suit and that we should have until 10 o'clock, "because," said he, "the servants will be at work in their homes until late and if they have any time for meeting they should have more time."

These are the names of the deacons: Brothers Daniel Murphy, Sr., Garrett Lamb, Henry Clay, George Kiser and Morgan Lewis. These and a few noble brethren and sisters began worship in an old plank stable, sitting just behind the present church. Since then the stable has been taken away. During our services the people would hold their umbrellas to protect themselves from the rains. I will say here, that while in this age of freedom and intellectual progress, looking back to those days of infancy of the Paris church, seeing how God has guided and blessed her and wiped from the country the stain of slavery which kept us from worshiping according to the Bible, in the midst of this great change in the affairs of church and State, I can say that "the people that sat in darkness have seen a great light."

It will not do to pass by the beginning of the Paris church without telling how the present compares with the past. Like the Savior, we began with a few, but out of that few many have come forth. In coming up through those years of struggle, many that started with me in the journey have fallen asleep in Christ and their bodies are sleeping in the grave, waiting the sound of the "trump of God." But since it is a fact a number of our brave soldiers have fallen from the field, there yet remain a number of veterans that sit with me in Zion and speak of the days when there was no colored Baptist church in Paris. Truly the Lord has been with us. We went on worshiping in the stable until we built a small house of worship. Finding that this would not accommodate us we tore it down and rebuilt, putting up the present building. I think we organized with fifty members. The church at that time being small they paid me $8 50 per trip from Maysville to Paris; and $6 50 of that I paid as my fare on the stage and fifty cents for two meals, one going and coming. I preached on in this way until the war, when they, seeing my necessities, agreed to pay me $29 15 per month, which price I have been getting since. As I was not a slave I had some difficulty in traveling. Frequently I would be riding among slaves that were hand-cuffed going south. The "negro traders" and other persons would ask me:

"Boy, where are you going?"

I would tell them to Paris.

"What for?" continued they.

Said I: "To preach."

"Does your master allow you to go from Maysville to Paris to preach?"

"Yes, sir."

"To whom do you belong?"

"I belong to Mr. Green."

"He must be a very good man."

Said I: "He is sir; a very good man."

The explanation of my belonging to Mr. Green is this: That I had, previous to this, bought myself from my master. I was now my own master. The wit comes in the expression, when they had asked to whom I belonged, I replied "to Mr. Green," meaning myself.

Another time, when going to Paris, I stopped at the Blue Licks, it being watering season, under the control of Mr. Thomas Holiday, who said that there were about five hundred persons from the south present, and I took dinner there as usual. When I had eaten I paid the steward and was out waiting for the stage. While standing on the steps I heard some one say "boy! boy!" and I turned. Said he: "Come here. Did you eat your dinner?" I told him that I did. "Who did you pay?" I told him that I had paid the steward. "Go and get the money from him." When I turned to go I met the steward. He handed Mr. Holiday the money which I had paid him. I then came out. He never charged me any more afterward. This was the result of being honest. He thought that I had slipped in there and eaten without having paid for it. At another time, when coming home from Paris, the bridge at the Blue Licks was burnt down. The stage had to ford the river. When we got across, and as there had been a temporary road cut, in walking up behind the passengers, I met two men. One appeared to be drunk. He came up to me and collared me. With an oath said he: "Where are you going?" I said nothing as yet. The other man said: "Let him alone, for he is a preacher." But, with another oath, he said that he would make me speak. I told him to take his hand out of my collar. He did not. I then knocked him about twenty feet backward. This was shortly after I had bought myself.

I will say that I was more of a slave after I bought myself than before. Before this I could go many places without interruption, but when I became a freeman I could not cross the Ohio river. Once, here in Maysville, I was summoned by the court for a witness in the trial of Burl and Spriggins. Isaac Spriggins, living with Billy and Nat. Poyntz, had a wife living at Dr. Shackleford's and so had Burl. From some cause Burl and Spriggins disagreed. Spriggins took up a small stove griddle and struck Burl in the head and broke a piece off in his head. The Poyntzes, who had him hired, were determined that Spriggins should not be hung. On the day of the trial I went to testify to Spriggins' character. I told them that when I first came to Maysville he was the first to put me in a way of making money. "Well," said they, "what do you know of his character?" I told them that he was a man with a passion, but if treated right would do most anything to assist you. He had often come over and assisted me and charged me nothing and I have done the same for him. They asked me what I knew about Burl.* I told them that I knew nothing of him scarcely, but was slightly acquainted with him, but that he was a man who drank whisky and that I never had anything to do with him whatever. Another lawyer asked me some question. I told him that I knew nothing of him because I never cared to know a man's bad traits except in cases of illustration, and that I loved no man better than I ought to. They told me to stand aside.

At this time my wife lived near Mayslick. I used to go out Saturdays on the stage and as the stage would never get down till Monday night I had to walk back. In coming through Washington, on several occasions, I was stopped for a runaway. I always carried with me a pair of saddle pockets in which I would carry things from Maysville to my wife and children. Mr. Payton, who was then a negro trader, hallooed at me, telling me to stop. I stopped. He asked me where I was going. I told him that I was going home. "Where do you live?" I told him that I lived at Mr. John P. Dobbyns'. He said that he thought that I was a runaway. I told him that I was just from my wife. He then asked to whom did my wife belong. I told him that she belonged to Mrs. Sissen. He said he had a great mind to put me in jail.†

"For," said he, "there was a negro that came along the other day and told such a tale as yours, and behold, he was a runaway."

I told him I did not care if he did put me in jail, "because," said

---

*It is well to say here that Burl, from effects of the stroke, died.

†The jail was then in Washington, which was at that time the County site.

I, "I am tired anyhow and if you can put me in jail I can get a rest."
I was tired because I had come a distance of eight miles.*

On another occasion, when coming through Washington, Conk
Owens stopped me.   He said that he believed that I was a runaway
also.   I told him that I wished John P. Dobbyns would publish me in
Washington so that they all would know me.   Saying this I walked on.
One night I had been out to prayer meeting.   At that time there were
night watches and they were empowered with the authority to whip any
negro they might catch out after 9 o'clock.   Stephen Lee was captain
of the watch, and him, I knew.   I think it was a little after 9, that I
was coming up the street and they stopped me, asking if I knew that
it was too late for me to be out.   I told them that I knew them and
would not run, because they would think that I was guilty of some
act.   With this explanation they let me go with threatenings of what
they would do should they catch me again.   I had been up to Sister
Jennie Marshall's to prayer meeting, as I was carrying on meeting at
her house once or twice a week.

Shortly after I joined the Mayslick Church, Alexander Campbell
and his doctrine had become very prominent and caused considerable
excitement among the Baptists.   Campbell's doctrine was, in substance,
"read, believe and be baptized."   Mr. Campbell and his doctrines
were met by the Rev. William Vaughan,† who was at that time a very
distinguished, energetic and prominent Baptist divine.   Mr. Vaughan,
indeed, defended the Baptist Church and faith with such eloquence,
with Biblical facts and from history, that many considered the doctrine
of Campbell nothing in his hands.   For the benefit of some that may
desire information on Campbellism, I will insert the following, which
may be found in the memoirs of Mr. Vaughan, written by his son.   In
speaking of Campbellism, he says:

1.   They, the Reformers, maintain that there is no promise of
salvation without baptism.

2.   That baptism should be administered to all that say they
believe that Jesus Christ is the son of God, without examination on any
other point.

3.   That there is no direct operation of the Holy Spirit on the
mind prior to baptism.

4.   That baptism procures the remission of sins and the gift of the
Holy Spirit.

---

*It is eight miles from Mayslick to Washington, and I had come from Mayslick.   I told him
that I could very patiently stay in jail till he sent word to Maysville.

† I have the memoirs of the Rev. Dr. Vaughan in my library.

5.   That the Scriptures are the only evidence of their interest in Christ.

6.   That obedience places it in God's power to elect to salvation.

7.   That no creed is necessary for the church, but the Scriptures as they stand.

8.   That all baptized persons have the right to administer the ordinance of baptism.

The writer continues: These resolutions were sent to the South Benson Church, Franklin County, Ky., where there was a considerable party in favor of Mr. Campbell, and after a lengthy discussion between George Waller on the one side and Jacob Creath, Sr., on the other, they were spread upon the records of the church.   The minority was so much incensed by this action that they met and with the assistance of Jacob Creath, Sr., and his nephew, Jacob Creath, Jr., constituted themselves into another church.   The majority regarding this matter as schismatic, at their regular meeting in February, 1830, unanimously excluded them from the Baptist Church, at South Benson.

This is sufficient proof as to the origin of Campbellism.   When the Baptists and Reformers split at Mayslick, Asa Runyon, Levi Vincamp, and Berry Dobbyns at this time used to preach (they were only elders of the church and not preachers) that if any man believed that Jesus Christ was the son of God and the Savior of sinners to come along and be baptized.   They also used to administer the supper. This is the begining of Campbellism.   I might say in closing this that Campbellism ever since its birth, has been met by our Baptist ministers very christianly and logically—and to-day though they have strayed from home, yet their mother, the Baptist Church, will accept them at any time.

While in a protracted meeting here in Maysville I was attacked by Mr. O——for keeping, as he said, late hours.   He afterward said that he did not mind the late hours so much as he did the hallooing of the people on the street.   He said that I had always broke up in reasonable time.   I then answered him.   I told him that he reminded me of Paul and Silas, when the woman had followed them for days.   Paul being grieved turned and commanded the evil spirit to come out of her. The masters, seeing that the hope of their gain was gone, had them put in prison, and when they brought them out to the magistrates said "These men do exceedingly trouble our nation, being Jews."   I said: "We are Baptists.   This is why we trouble you."   And further, I told him that he reminded me of a fox that was at his devilment and got his tail cut off and in order not to be disgraced, called the rest of the foxes and got them all to cut their tails off, and when he did this his devilment was hid.

CHAPTER III.

A T one time the Rev. Mr. Fisher protracted a meeting here in the Methodist church for about six weeks. At the close of the meeting, having been very successful, he said that all who wanted to remain members of the Methodist Church could do so and those that wanted to be Baptists could be the same.

The following ministers have been pastors of the white Baptist Church since I have been in Maysville: Rev. Walter Warder, Rev. Gilbert Mason, Rev. Thomas G. Keen, Rev. W. W. Gardner, Rev. Joseph W. Warder, D. D., Rev. George Hunt, Rev. Henry Ray, Rev. J. M. Bennett, Rev. F. W. Stone, Rev. A. W. Chamliss, D. D., Rev. J. M. Frost. D. D., Rev. George Varden, Ph.D., Rev. S. L. Helm, D. D., Rev. J. K. Pace and Rev. R. B. Garrett.

At this time, the Baptists had no regular preacher, and I would frequently visit the Presbyterian Church (white.) On one occasion, the Rev. R. C. Grundy, pastor in charge, after concluding his discourse, said that he was authorized by the Synod of Kentucky to open his church once a month for the purpose of preaching to the colored people of Maysville. This of course would prevent us from having meeting. One of the white churches would be opened each Sabbath for the express purpose of preaching to the colored people. Henry Johnson, a colored Methodist preacher, had gone to Cincinnati on account of the "Fugutive Slave Law," and had returned to Maysville again on a visit to see his father, who lived in the town of Washington. Mr. Grundy, the Presbyterian preacher, said this way of suffering preachers to come from Cincinnati and to go up on that hill and preach to the colored people would not do, "for," continued he, "who knows what they are preaching into them?" Andrew Thomas, another Methodist, Harry Smith and myself were sitting in the gallery of the church listening to Mr. Grundy's remarks. At the close of the meeting, when we had come out, I said to Thomas and Smith: "We ought not to stand such expressions as Mr. Grundy made this morning. We should meet and write him a letter and let him know that what he said is not true." So they agreed to my proposition to write him a letter contradicting what he (Mr. Grundy) had said in the pulpit concerning our people. We agreed to do so the next week. When the time came both of them backed down. I then told them that I would write to him, if I lost all my reputation afterward. I went to Mr. J. M. Stockton, who was our Commission Clerk, and who also did all of my writing. By the way, he was a gentleman. I told him that after supper I wanted him to write for me a letter. He said that when he had finished eating he would do so. He got ready and began writing; when he had written awhile, he stopped and told me that he was afraid to write that because they knew his handwriting. He then asked what I was going to do with it, and if I was going to put it in the postoffice. I told him that I was not, and that I was going to give it to Mr. Grundy from my hand and tell him what it was. Upon this proposition, he wrote it and sealed it up. The Courthouse had just been built and Mr. Grundy had obtained it for the purpose of preaching to the colored people, as he had said. I went down in town and met him on Third street, near the Courthouse. I was watching for him anyway. Jerry Anderson had a chair carrying it into the Courthouse for Mr. Grundy to sit in. When Mr. Grundy came up, I spoke to him and told him that I had a letter that I was going to give him and wished him to read it and give me an answer to it. I gave him the letter and left him. I never received an answer and he never preached to the colored people any more on that line. He said afterwards that he never knew that we had a house of worship and then we were worshiping in the old frame church which stands behind the new. So this was the last of the white churches being opened in which to preach to the colored people.

When Palmer, of Louisville, was giving out passes, he sent an agent here with the authority to give passes to any that desired. My daughter Amanda, who was owned by Mr. John C. Reid, went to the agent, got a pass and came home to me. A day or two afterwards Mr. Reid came to my house. He told me that I must send Amanda home, and that I was harboring slaves I told him that I would not do any such thing. He then turned and went out. The next morning he came again with his son and asked me the same questions as before. I still contended that I would not send her back. He said no more but went and got out a warrant for me for "harboring slaves." I employed Mr. Sulser as the lawyer for me. At the appointed day for trial I came up. When the examination of witnesses was finished Mr. Reid's lawyer made a speech. When he got through the judge told my lawyer that it was useless for him to speak, for his mind was already made up that I should pay the damages, which were $30. The Sheriff came to me and asked whether I had any money with which to pay my fine. I told him that I had none. He then asked who I would get to go my security. I told him "Nobody." He then told me that I must go to jail. I told him very well that I would go and tell Mr. Grant to put me in and he needed not to go with me. I left the Sheriff by the Courthouse, and when I got a little beyond the Presbyterian Church, he said "O d—n it, come back."

I came back and we went up into the Courthouse together. When we had been there a little time, he went to some one and whispered, I told them that the whole thing was rascality, a cheat and fraud. They then told me that I might go home. I went to Mr. Larrel, the head of the Bureau, and told to him the whole case. He told me to go back and get my lawyer to write the proceedings of the trial. I asked Mr. Sulser, the lawyer, what he would charge to write out the proceedings of het trial. He told me $5. I told him to go ahead and write them. I took them to Captain Larrel and he sent them to Louisville to General Palmer. I do not think they were gone over two days before they came back forbidding them to touch anything that I owned. Captain Larrell told me to stand on the street that I might see the Sheriff and if he said anything to me, that I must send him to him. I went to the place designated. The Sheriff saw me and called me to him. I went to him. He asked me if I had that money yet. I told him "No sir, I have not." I told him that Captain Larrell desired to see him. He asked me what Captain Larrell knew about it. I told him that I did not know, but he told me to tell you. He went and Captain Larrell forbid him touching anything of mine. He told him to go and see Reid and try and get him to compromise with me. He went and saw Reid and came back. I was still on the street, for I knew what was going to be done. The Sheriff seeing me, told me I had better go around and see Reid. I got Brother William Rudd, who is a consistant member of my church in Maysville at present, and went out. When I got there Mr. Reid spoke very politely. I returned to him the compliment. I told him that I had come to see about my daughter, Amanda. He said that he thought that it was settled, but that he concluded to relinquish the principal providing that I would pay the cost.

I told him that I would have to go to the Courthouse and find what the cost was. The cost was $7. Before I paid I went to see Captain Larrell. He told me that if I were to carry it to the United States Court I might get justice done me there. But the prejudice was so great here against our people that if he were I, he would pay the cost and have nothing more to do with it. I did so and the case was dropped. One morning very early I heard a noise at the door, and upon hearing, I went to the door. I opened the door, and behold! there stood my daughter Maria with a bundle of clothes lying near her. I asked her what was the matter. She said that she had left home and was not going back any more. I told her to come in. Mrs. Dobbyns, finding that she had gone, sent for me to come down there. I went down according to request. When I got there she told me that I must send Maria home. I told her I would do no such thing, but if Maria wanted to come she could do so. Then said they if she does not she will have to leave the state. I told them very well; I would never send her back. George Ore, her son-in-law, went down to the boat with us. When we got to the river the Captain of the ferry-boat would not permit her to cross because Ore did not own her. Mr. Ore had been instructed by Mrs. Dobbyns to take Maria and send her across the river. The captain told him if he would go back and get permission from the city Mayor that he would take her over. In coming from the river he was so angry that he replied that he wished every negro was in hell. When we had gotten over the river, in passing by a warehouse, Dr. Moore, of Aberdeen, who was a Republican and a good man, saw us and came out from the warehouse and asked what was the matter. I told him that my daughter Maria got her clothes and came home and they told her that if she did not come back she would have to leave the state. The doctor told us to wait. He went down to Mrs. Dennis, his daughter, and told her to keep Maria until I could get a place for her.

Caroline, another of my daughters, belonged to Robert Andrews. She wanted to leave but was afraid. A squad of soldiers went there and got her. I went down and took her to Portsmouth, O. From there I took the train and went up to Jackson, about twenty miles above Portsmouth. I left Caroline with her sister Charlotte.

CHAPTER IV.

O NCE upon an occasion I preached upon the subject of "Baptism." And as the Methodists were opposed to us having the church, some of them told Mr. Grundy that Mr. Mason, who was then pastor of the white Baptist Church, had been to our church and preached on baptism. But the statement was not true. Mr. Grundy accepted an invitation from the Methodists to preach for them, intending to answer Mr. Mason, of whom it was said that he preached in our church. He made an appointment. When the time came I went to hear him answer Mr. Mason.* When he had concluded his remarks he read a hymn and gave it to Robert Lawson who, being unable to sing it, handed it to Jerry Anderson. Jerry being in the same fix as Lawson, gave it to me and I sang it. When he had dismissed the people I called his attention to the commission. I told him that I understood the commission to be: "Go into the world and preach the gospel to every creature; he that believeth and is baptised shall be saved." And that I wanted him to tell me whether or not I was right. He said that he concurred with me most heartily, and besides that he never admitted to the communion table any unbaptised person. When I came out the congregation said had I not spoken I would have bursted.

Henry Lee was then sexton of the white Presbyterian Church, of which Mr. Grundy was pastor. At night Mr. Grundy preached, and also told Mr. Lee, the sexton, that he was told that it was not Mr. Mason that preached the sermon on baptism, but it was Green. "I will not preach for those negroes any more." Mr. Grundy had been much mistaken about the preacher of that sermon, for it was I myself. About this time Mr. Frost was holding a meeting in the white Baptist Church, of which I was sexton. It was in the winter season. Then I generally sat below to attend to the fires. Mr. Mason, the pastor, had

---

* It was not Mr. Mason that had preached the sermon on baptism but it was I.

gone to the country to marry a couple. There was a gentleman that came up to join the church. Mr. Frost said: "Friend, tell us your object in coming forward." Said he: "I want to join the church." "Do you love the people of God?" "Yes, as far as I can see them." At this time, Mr. Kirk, a deacon, told Mr. Frost to postpone his admittance until the pastor came, which, he said, would be the next night. Mr. Frost then asked the gentleman if he would be there the next night. He said: "No, if you don't take me now I will never be here any more." I was sexton nearly sixteen years and I never saw him there any more.

I was very anxious to get a set of silver spoons. I will say in the outset that the way I obtained them I scraped them up off the floor. One year there was a failure in the crops. In the fall the people drove their hogs to the mountains and fed them on the "mast." As I was living in the "commission house," the following year we bought up a great deal of bacon. The river fell so that it was impossible to ship anything, and buying so much bacon that in order to place it all we had to pile it up about six feet high. The weight of this pressed out so much oil we would put down sawdust to keep it from running over the floor. Every morning my work was to change the old sawdust and put down new. In looking at it I found that there was much grease in it. The summer being hot and dry I wondered if there was not some way by which that grease could be gotten out. Thinking a while, I got an empty nail keg, filled it full of greasy sawdust and turned it bottom upwards on two sticks across a kettle. I kept on in this way until I got nearly a barrel of grease. Mr. Ford, a soap-maker, who sold his soap in our warehouse, came in one day and I showed it to him. He told me to send it to the soap factory. I did so and he sent me soap to the amount of $37. I cashed it to the warehouse, which paid me the amount named above. I took the $37 to the silversmith, Mr. Boyd, and told him to make for me a half dozen dessert spoons and the same number of tea spoons. Mr. Boyd did as I requested. I have the spoons to-day. You can now see my reason for saying that I scraped my silver spoons from the floor. At another time when we had received 500 or 600 kegs of nails, and in rolling them from the gangway of the boat they let five of them fall into the river. The warehouse would not receive them in this condition. So they told me if I would clean and dry them they would give me $1 per keg. I got my kettle in which I had the grease before. After studying awhile, I took it out into the back yard and built a big fire under it. When it got hot I put the wet nails into it.

putting at the same time a little cold water with them. When I took
them out they were just like they were before they had fallen in the
river. I was not over an hour cleaning five kegs. I went in and told
them that I was through with the nails. Some of them did not believe
me until they went out and saw. When they saw it was so they gave
me $5. After this some of them at the warehouse told me that they
would give me twenty-five cents per dozen for all the rats I could catch
there. Indeed the rats were bad there. I went up in the third story
and studied a plan upon which to work. I made me some old-fashioned triggers and set them baited with hemp seed and dried beef.
Sometimes of mornings I would go up there and would find eight or
nine rats. In this way I would catch so many that they got tired of
paying for them.

By this time the emancipation of the colored people by President
Lincoln had added to my family three more of my children. My wife
had lost an eye from a spell of sickness that she had when a slave. She
could only use one hand. In order to pay for my house and clothe my
family I must, of necessity, get to some trade. I by some chance did
some work for Mrs. Arthur Berry. When I was through she told me
that I must whitewash her kitchen, yard fences and outhouses. I told
her that I knew nothing about whitewashing. She told me to get the
lime and she would show me. I did so and she showed me as she
said. When I was through she paid me just as if I had been an old
whitewasher. By this I saw I could make money. I next did some
whitewashing for Mr. Shultz, a very prominent citizen of Maysville. I
did a great deal for him—was there over a month. He had a receipt
from Washington City for whitewashing—to make all colors. When I
got through he gave it to me. I then fell in company with Mr. James
Smith, a painter. I would frequently work with him. I learned a
great deal of the trade. In going around to whitewash I would get hold
of many chairs that needed bottoms. As cane bottoms were not so
much in fashion as now most of the ladies preferred "shuck" bottoms.
I would gather a number of chairs that needed bottoms. My four girls,
my son and myself would at times be working on a chair apiece. The
regular price for a "shuck" bottom was fifty cents. In this way, with
my four children, I would make $3 per day. I then bought me a set
of shoemaker's tools. I would fix my family's shoes. By this I learned
the trade very well. I kept on till I could cut and make shoes. I
learned how to make brooms also. People in the country would bring
me their broom-corn and I would make brooms "one half for the

other." I also bought a set of carpenter's tools. I tried, as the saying is, to be a "jack of all trades." Shortly after this, when in Paris, I learned that a great many colored people had been driven from their masters and had come to Paris for protection. A great many crowded into an old stable rented to them at $10 per month. I went in there and saw a cooking stove and saw that they used the hole in the stable, from which the horse could get light, for a chimney.

Samuel H. Clay had a field to sell—the spot where Claysville is now. He fenced it in and wanted to make of it a shipping pen. The city would not consent. He then ran it off in lots of seventy-five by sixty feet. At this time Elder Henry Lighter was pastor at the Methodist Episcopal Church. Mr. Clay finding that the city objected to him making of it a shipping pen, determined to sell the lots to the colored people. He sent a proposition to Mr. Lighter and he in turn sent it back to Mr. Clay, with the expression that his business was to preach the gospel and not to attend to political matters. Mr. Clay told me this from his own mouth, and it is not hearsay. The following Sabbath being my day in Paris Mr. Clay sent for me. I went to see him according to request. When I went in and was seated he told me that he had a proposition to make to me. He said he had some lots to sell and the terms of the sale are these: That the lots were seventy-five by sixty feet and that he would build upon that a cottage, with one door and chimney, for $500 cash, or $100 down with 6 per cent. interest, and when paid for would give the deed. He said that he sent the same proposition to Mr. Lighter and he refused it. "And now," said Mr. Clay to me, "what do you think of it?" I told him that his proposition was a good one and it would suit the necessities of my people at present. And furthermore, I told him that I thought it as much my duty to look after the interests of my people as to preach the gospel, for that to some extent is a part of the gospel.

"Well," said Mr. Clay, "here is the proposition and if your people agree to it, tell them to meet me on the lot at 10 o'clock to-morrow."

When I had finished preaching on Lord's day I told my congregation why I thought they should accept Mr. Clay's proposition, and the whole church voted to meet him on the lot Monday morning. By 12 o'clock Monday Mr. Clay had sold fifty or sixty lots. So I was the first to put the colored people of Paris in the way of purchasing to themselves property. For my influence in this matter Mr. Clay presented me, by my own choosing, a nice hat. He told me to go to the store and pick out such a hat as I wanted, and I did so.   You can judge that it was a good one.

In 1864 I left home with the intention of going to Louisville.   I got as far as Cincinnati.   Elder Shelton, being in a series of meetings, would not consent for me to leave.   I staid with him a week.   The people of Cincinnati were so well pleased and the meeting seemed to be in such good prospects that they contended that I should stay longer. By so doing I was delayed in my trip to Louisville.   When I got to Louisville Brother Adams said that he had been looking for me on nearly every boat.   I staid some considerable time with him and left for home.   At this time I was beginning to be prominent among the ministers of the state.   My first associates as ministers were Charles Threlkeld, of Maysville; London Ferrel, of Lexington; Henry Adams, of Louisville; George W. Dupee, of Paducah; Henry Green, of Danville; Matt. Campbell, of Richmond; Henry Evans, of Lexington; R. Lee, of Georgetown; Isaac Slaughter, of Danville; R. Martin, of Frankfort; Tobias Smith, of Stamping Ground, and Garrett Reid, of Paris.

In 1865 I was called to Louisville again by the Rev. H. Adams for the pupose of organizing a convention to take in consideration the propriety of fixing some plan for the education of the rising generation. The majority of those I have just mentioned were there for the same purpose.   When we had go ten there the body was organized into a Convention of Colored Baptist Ministers of the State of Kentucky, being also the first body of colored Baptist ministers ever assembled in the state.   The Rev. Henry Adams, pastor of the Fifth-street Church, and who was the prime mover in the matter, was made President. Brothers Peter Smith, John Thomas and Tabb Smith, of Frankfort, took an active part in the proceedings of the convention.   In this convention we agreed to purchase the "Hill property," at Frankfort, for the purpose of erecting thereon a college in order to educate our people and get a competent and well educated ministry.   We saw from our own ability, and looking at the condition of our people just from slavery, that our effort to do this was a good one.   Brother Adams, possessing a more competent education than many of us, was recognized as a kind of leader in the matter.   When the question of educating the coming generation was proposed the convention seemed to have caught a new spirit of enthusiasm.   We old brethren just out of slavery, many of us not having had the privilege to learn, thought it a grand thing to build an educational structure upon which, when we were dead, our children would look with pride and call us "blessed." Many of those pioneers who were prime movers in the educational work of the race, and who used every thing necessary to the advancement of the Baptist cause in the state, have fallen to "sleep with their fathers."

Here and there we can possibly find one. What a change in the last twenty years! No body of men were more anxious or assembled more interested in what was before them. I sometimes get vexed at our young brethren now in the associations. They will meet at a place on Wednesday and stay all the week and nothing done—so many points of order and other technical things that might be let alone. The convention of that date was not possessed of the amount of brain and education as the associations of to-day, but they did business in a more intelligent and systematic style than our present associations. I speak more exclusively of the General Association. The convention knew what it came there to do and the time in which it was to be done. They knew that opportunities misused could not be had again. These things pushed us to the mark of our great work. There is indeed a great change in our delegation of to-day from what there was then. In this age there is entirely too much levity among the ministers—too much of those things practiced which, when viewed from a Christian standpoint, tend to bring about what I call a "false ministry." In those times, when the delegates would become somewhat unconcerned in the work of the convention, Elder Adams would tell them to finish business and then play. "Let us do our work first, and if there be any spare time afterwards, we will use it in play." It was a pleasure to me then to visit and meet my brethren. They seemed to be in union about the work they had come to perform. Where the spirit of God is there is peace and harmony, both of purpose and action. If in those days of illiteracy and limited education it took the spirit of God to bless our work, it takes the same now. Having held a pleasant session all the week everybody seemed to be pleased with our visit, and when the time came to go home—that is for the delegates to return to their respective fields of labor—the people would look as if they carried a burden of sorrow; and the delegates would weep much because of their separation. But now the preachers do so much rascality the people are glad when the Association adjourns.

As I said, we agreed to purchase the property at Frankfort. This property was composed of about fifty acres of land situated in Frankfort. In order to purchase this property the churches were taxed from $50 to $100 each, to be paid annually till the debt was paid. I being pastor of two churches, Maysville and Paris, would take $100; that is,

$50 from each church. This shows whether or not I have done anything for the college. I have been branded as sitting still and doing nothing for the college. This money was for the purpose of paying for the property. Such churches as Fifth Street, Louisville, and Green Street, and First Church, Lexington, would send up $100 for this purpose. We continued in this way till the property was ours. I said then, and do say yet, that the Association made a great big mistake when it sold that property. I have no objections to Louisville, but simply to save money; for had the same property been in Louisville I would have not been less interested. This was ours and all we had to do was to build upon it. We could, in my estimation, very easily have done so. But the act has been done and reflection cannot change it.

This property having been sold, the General Association purchased the present property in Louisville, and five or six years ago opened a school with the Rev. W. J. Simmons, D.D., President. Dr. Simmons has been of use to the Baptists of the state. He is a clear-headed, influential and progressive little man. He will do the Baptist cause much good. He deserves much credit for what he has done in the last six years to cultivate our young men and women. God grant that the university under his care may do much good; that it will not be long until there shall have gone forth from the walls men and women qualified for any good work.

The second Baptist Convention met with the Baptist Church of Frankfort. The third Baptist Convention met with the First Baptist Church of Lexington. I preached the introductory sermon from the fifteenth chapter of the Book of Exodus, and the eleventh verse. In this convention the name was changed to that of General Association of Colored Baptists of Kentucky. As this is not intended to be a history of the colored Baptists of Kentucky I shall be obliged to leave the meetings and proceedings of our Associations. I would be glad to speak of each annual session from its organization to the present but my memory will not allow it. In 1855 I visited the Rev. Henry Adams again. I staid with him three weeks. The meeting resulted in many converts. The Sunday night he baptized I concluded to leave for home. Monday morning I came down from my room with the intention of leaving for home. Elder Adams met me at the steps and asked if I were crazy. I told him that I was going home. He told me that I was not going, for he wanted me to preach at night for him again. He had given me $30. I considered the matter and concluded to stay and preach. I preached for him at night as requested. After preaching he told me to come down on the platform, that he wanted them to understand that he had labored with me in more satisfaction than any other minister he ever did labor with. He told the congregation that he had kept me from going home and all that wished to give me anything for staying to come forward and put it into my hands. I think they gave me $6 and over. At another time I visited the Green-street Baptist Church. Elder Shanks, I think, was preaching for them. The church was in a little difficulty about something which I do not now remember. I recollect helping him in trying to settle it. I would frequently visit the Rev. Henry Adams after the first time. Elder Adams died in Louisville about fourteen years ago—I think it was in November of 1873. He was a fine Christian gentleman—always willing and ready for any good work which would be of use to the Baptists and the race generally. The Rev. Andrew Heath survives him as pastor and shepherd of the flock of God. O, for more such men!

On one occasion I rode from Paris to Maysville, sitting in the stage with two gentlemen who were discussing the "Foreknowledge of God." They had been talking on the subject for some time. One of them turned to me and said, very politely: "Old man, are you a preacher?" I told him I went for that. He said that he wished to ask me a question. I told him that I had no objections whatever. He proceeded then with his question:

"When God made Adam and put him into the garden did he know that Adam would sin?"

I told him "Yes."

"I want you to tell me why God let Adam sin and then punished him?"

This is the answer that I gave him: "God never made Adam a slave, but a free agent."

I do not think that before this I had once thought of the subject. I visited Paducah to assist the Rev. G. W. Dupee in a meeting. While I was there many were added to the church—I do not remember the exact number. During the days of slavery I was frequently invited by the white folks to preach the funerals of their dead slaves. But the law would not suffer it without some white person present. I frequently had as many whites in my audience as colored.*

The church at Washington, which was built by Mr. George Orr, got in debt and was unable to pay it. Mr. Orr told me that if I did

*This should have been mentioned before, but I do not think it out of place to mention just here.

not go to Washington and raise him $30 he would sell the church to the Irish. I took my church and went up there and raised the money and paid the debt and they were bothered no more. I also took up the first money for the Lewisburg Baptist Church, of which the Rev. C. Davis, of Cynthiana, is pastor. In 1872 Brother Milton Foster put into my hands $6 85 for the purpose of buying a lot. In 1873 the sexton of the Lewisburg Church gave me $1, which I held till the next year. I chartered the train and took my church out to Lewisburg and took up a reasonable sum of money. I put this money into the hands of Brother Thomas Calvert. Brother Calvert held it till the lot was purchased. So I took up the first money in order to build the church at Lewisburg. They have a good house of worship and number about sixty-five. A little before this I induced the Rev. L. C. Natas to go out in the region of Mayslick. The church there had been under Elder John Marcum. But during the war it had gone back considerably. Elder Natas went there and began a meeting. He preached on the farm of Mr. Shanklin till he took in a certain number of converts. When I heard this Dr. Helm, Elder Bagby and myself met in council and ordained Brother Natas to the gospel ministry. The Rev. Dr. Helm preached the sermon of ordination. I then went out to Mr. Shanklin's and preached for Elder Natas also. The following Sabbath Elder Natas baptized. He went to Mayslick and preached there awhile and built a church. During the building of that and making the contract with the carpenters they disagreed. He then locked up the house and came after me. I appointed a day and took my church up there and took up enough money to get the house opened. Every since they have been going on under the pastorates of Rev. L. C. Natas, the Rev. D. B. Green and the Rev. R. Strauss, respectively.

About this time Elder Natas began preaching in Sharpsburg. When he had preached there awhile I went up and organized a church of which the Rev. G. W. Canada, of Mt. Sterling, is pastor. About the same time I organized a church in Mt. Sterling. I also assisted the Rev. Thomas Taylor, of Clintonville, the Centreville Baptist Church, under the Rev. Thomas Gant, of Lexington, and Leesburg Church, under the Rev. J. H. Lewis, now of Washington, Ky.

In January, after the emancipation of the slaves, I told the brethren that the Lord had in reservation for us a blessing. I then expressed my feelings in starting a series of meetings. We began an inquiry meeting, which lasted a week. Everything went on very agreeably till I went to Paris and came back. I felt as soon as I came back that there was something wrong in the church. So the next night Brother William Smith made a statement that he was greatly grieved at the manner in which Brother Alex. Stewart had treated him Sunday morning, and Brother Smith told the conversation that passed between them. Brother Stewart acknowledged that he did so and that it was wrong. They then made up and gave each other his hand. So the meeting went on, I having no help, but did the preaching myself. And laboring very hard, I found myself weakening. I went to Paris and secured the assistance of the Rev. Clay, of Xenia, O. He came and preached a few nights and gave out. I paid him and he went home. The meeting closed. I was sick afterwards for some weeks, the physicians attending me daily. They put me under the influence of chloroform. When they began operating I commenced preaching. My wife and children rushed up in the room, supposing that they were killing me. I was so ill that my wife wrote to my son Marshall to come home at once, that his father was so low that he was liable to die at any time. She also sent another letter to the brethren of Paris. Two of them came down. Finding that I was better they turned their visit into a prayer meeting. God was merciful toward me and I was permitted to rise again. When I had been well a few days we began another meeting, which resulted in sixty or seventy-five souls. The first baptizing succeeding this revival, I baptized in the Ohio river twenty-five; at the next, about a week afterwards, fifteen. At other times five and six, two, three, &c. Brother Lewis Lightfoot, of Washington, came and preached a week. Brother Lightfoot thought, I suppose, that they had been joining a little too fast, so finally he preached a sermon to let them know if they had been deceived in their profession of faith in Christ. The congregation gave him $7 and a few cents and he left and never came back any more.

CHAPTER V.

SOME time after this I went to the Courthouse to listen to a speech delivered in regard to the election and my race especially. The speaker was a Democrat. In the course of his speech he said that he did not believe the negro was human; that he was of a species between the baboon and the monkey; that God had foreordained that he should be a slave. He then tried to substantiate his pernicious, cowardly and mean statements. He asked what the negro had invented. He said nothing but an old banjo. Who wishes the negro sitting in their parlor beside their daughters? or, to use the express words of the speaker: "How would it look for a great, big, black negro buck sitting beside your daughter?" These are his exact words. A few nights afterwards the Republicans had a kind of jubilee. I was sitting there listening very contentedly, when Mr. Wadsworth came and told me that I must go up and make a speech. I thanked him kindly for the invitation and at the same time expressed my inability to do so. He insisted that I should go up and say something, if nothing more than "I am a Republican, from head to foot." So finally I concluded to go up with him. When I got up there I thanked, in a brief way, the gentleman for the invitation and began my speech by referring to the speech of the Democrat previous to that. I told them that I was over fifty years old and the next Monday I would be twenty-one.*

I told them that the Democratic speaker told them the other night that I was of a species between the baboon and the monkey. You know it is customary for those animals to have tails. Had I a tail next Monday I would quirl it upon my back and go to the polls and vote the Republican ticket. While the crowd was cheering I came down.

---

*By saying that I would be twenty-one I meant to convey the idea that the next Monday would be the first time I was recognized as a qualified voter or citizen of the United States. The law requires a man to be twenty-one in order to vote.

At another time, when speaking down on Front street, I told the Democrats that any party that was in favor of a law which made a man dishonest I thought that party was wrong. The law, in substance, was that no difference how much money I had when a slave, I could not buy myself. The law said further that if any man is a slave he cannot buy himself. With $600 in my pocket I could not buy my own sister unless the "bill of sale" was made out in mother's name. She herself was compelled to own slaves to get my sister's freedom. I had the money to buy myself when I was a slave, but the "bill of sale" was made out in my mother's name. The party that made this law is dishonest. I told them that there were in Canada men and women. Had it not been that such an outrageous and dishonest law existed here those men and women would be here to-day. At this saying I concluded and left.

I was chosen by the colored citizens of this place to represent them in the first convention of colored men ever assembled in the state. This convention met in Lexington in the year 1866. It is not my intention to make you think I am a politician. Those who know me can judge of the fact. Politics and I are not related, only so far as it becomes my duty to advise my people to look to their own interests. That convention was a grand gathering of colored men just from bondage. It held a session of three days. For the benefit of some who wish to know its object in meeting I will insert here a synopsis of its proceedings. This may benefit some young man in his efforts to become famous in politics. I will present the resolutions and the grand memorial to Congress. A certain paper, from which I cut this, spoke as follows:

The following are the remainder of the proceedings of the Colored People's Convention that closed on Thursday:

Resolved, That we appoint the Hon. M. C. Johnson. Willard Davis and William Brown to represent us at Frankfort and lay before the General Assembly of Kentucky the necessities and requirements of the colored people.

Resolved, That we appoint the Hon. W. C. Goodloe and General James Brisbin to represent us at Washington and lay before the Congress of the United States the necessities and requirements of the colored people.

WHEREAS, Several of the journals opposed to the enfranchisement of the colored man have, from patriotic motives, boldly come forward and advocated their rights of testimony in the courts, therefore,

Resolved, That we tender them our thanks in this matter of advocating the cause of justice. Also be it

Resolved, That the Louisville *Courier*, Lexington *Observer*, Lexing ton *Statesman*, Frankfort *Commonwealth* and all the Republican journals that have so no nobly stood up for the right have our respect and warmest thanks.

Resolved, That we authorize Willard Davis, Dr. A. M. Davidson and W. J. Butler additional representatives of our claims in Congress.

The following were elected as officers of the convention:

President—W. J. Butts.

Vice President—D. V. Higdon.

Secretary—R. W. T. James, of Frankfort.

Assistant Secretary—V. H. Gibson, of Louisville.

Treasurer—James Turner, of Lexington.

Sergeant-at-arms—Henry Scroggins, of Lexington.

The Committee on Education made their report, as follows:

Having long felt the need of education among the 4,000,000 of freedmen of the south, and having learned that such a need is being met by a National Reform Association, conducted by the leading colored men of the country, its headquarters being at the city of New Albany, therefore,

Resolved, That we hail with delight and heartily commend its aims and purposes to our citizens throughout the land.

This was the memorial to Congress adopted:

To the Honorable House of Representatives and the Senate of the United States in Congress Assembled: The colored people of Kentucky, through their delegates in convention assembled, most respectfully petition your honorable body to grant us the right of suffrage. Your petitioners beg leave to call your attention to the fact that they are not allowed to testify in the courts of the commonwealth against white persons, and that, in consequence, many persons who commit murder, rape, arson and all manner of outrages upon the colored people are permitted to go unpunished. Your petitioners would further say that they are now and ever have been loyal to the Government of the United States; more than 30,000 of their brothers and sons enlisted in the late war: that they are peaceable, law-abiding citizens, who pay taxes as other people, but on the account of the color of their skins, are denied political rights in the government which they support. Your petitioners would further say that inasmuch as the constitution of the United States has abolished slavery everywhere within its jurisdiction, so that all constitutions, laws or regulations growing out of the same are null and void; and inasmuch as the same constitution in another provision declares that no state shall make or enforce any laws which shall abridge the privilege or immunities of citizens of the United States; and inasmuch as Congress is empowered by appropriate legislation to enforce these several provisions, which we believe cannot be done without securing the elective franchise to citizens of color; and inasmuch as the color of our skin did not in the time of war prevent the government from claiming our allegiance and causing us to bear arms in its defense, and it is a well established principle of just government that allegiance and protection go together, the one being the consideration of the other, and inasmuch as the Declaration of Independence promises the equality of the people, and it is the express duty of Congress under the constitution to guarantee to every state in the Union a republican form of government; and inasmuch as many white persons of no greater degree of intelligence than we are allowed to vote in this commonwealth, and thousands of them fought against the government in the late war; and inasmuch as we desire to assist the Unionists of the state in electing loyal men to office, now, therefore, we do earnestly pray your honorable body, in such way and manner as it may legally and properly be done, to enact such laws or amend the constitution so as to secure to every citizen in this commonwealth who may have been a slave, or is the descendant of a slave, or by reason of race or color is deprived of equal rights to vote at all elections for members of Congress, for Presidential electors, for Representatives and Senators of the Legislature of the State, for all State, city, town and officers of all kinds, upon the same terms and considerations as white citizens, and we pray the blessings of God upon your deliberations.

This concludes the address to the United States Congress. The convention also sent an address to the General Assembly of Kentucky, which was as follows:

To the General Assembly of the Commonwealth of Kentucky: The colored people of the commonwealth of Kentucky, through their delegates in convention assembled, most respectfully petition your honorable body to so alter and amend the clause of the statutes as to permit no person to be disqualified from giving his testimony in any of the courts of the commonwealth, in actions both civil and criminal by reason of birth, color or previous condition. We also most respectfully state that any and all obligations to this much needed reform are based upon the theory that our juries are honest enough to render their verdict to and in accordance with the law and the evidence, and that they have intelligence enough to discriminate between conflicting statements, to detect falsehood, to arrive at the truth of every case and render impartial justice between man and man. Unless this theory is true—and no one asserts to the contrary—the judiciary system of the state is a failure. If true, when applied to white people, it must, by every sound system of reasoning, be true when applied to us. To say that a jury of white men, upon their oaths are honest enough to do justice between white men and intelligent enough to decide upon truthfulness of statements made to it by such evidence, and, at the same time too dishonest to do justice between a white man and black one and has not intelligence to decide upon their truthfulness, is an assertion too absurd for utterance, and is an insult to every right minded man; that this is the logical argument to be deduced from this our present system. If your juries are competent to make their verdicts under the law from the evidence of white persons, they are equally competent to do so from the evidence of

black persons.   Some may say that we are incompetent to serve as witnesses in cases where a white person is an interested party, by
reason of our want of intelligence or our disregard of truth.   We
deny this most emphatically.   The same objections may extend
to thousands of white persons in this state.   Juries almost daily
render verdicts directly opposite the statement of some witnesses in whose testimony they have no confidence, and many a white
man is a witness whose intelligence is no greater than a black man.
These are matters that should not be urged against a class of witnesses
white or black.   It surely occurs that false testimony escapes alike
the attention of the court, the jury, the clients and attorneys engaged
in trial and a rigid enforcement of the law, punishing perjury, will
protect society from all this of character.   Under our law we are competent clients and witnesses against each other.   In action, both civil
and criminal, when our own people are interested, in property or life,
we are citizens of the same common country.   Much of the property
now constituting the aggregate wealth of Kentucky has been acquired
or improved by our labor.   None know better than the citizens of this
State how we have protected and cared for both the property and lives
of those of our former owners.   Suddenly freed by act of war we were
mostly thrown upon our own resources, without property or means of
protecting what little we now have, which is the product of our own toil
and care.   It is larceny to steal it from us; it is murder to feloniously de-
prive one of our people of his life.   Is there a member of your honorable
body who would offer inducement to crime, outrage and lawlessness by
saying that the white man's property and the white man's life are protected under our law, but the property and life of a blackman is
unworthy of protection and beyond the pale of our law?   We hope
not; but this is what the law now says.   We can be despoiled of our
property, our females may be outraged, our school teachers shot down
at their desks, our ministers murdered in their pulpits by any person
lawless enough to do so.   The sad history of the past few years must
convince you that many men, though lawless, live in Kentucky and
we have no remedy in the courts, if the only witness have African
blood in his veins. no matter how truthful or intelligent he may be.
On many of the lonely farms of our state, in the absence of the owner,
his wife and daughter are the only white persons remaining.   His
property may be stolen, his wife and daughter may be outraged and
murdered during his absence, in the presence of every colored servant
on the place, by a white man, and the villian goes unpunished because
the witnesses are black.   We believe that much good will accrue to
both races when this right is given to our people.   Society will be
more protected from crime than it is now.   We do not expect by our
rights of testimony to influence wrongfully the action of any court or
jury, but simply desire the right of any of our people to go before any
court or jury and testify upon cases of law as any other people.   And
that equal and exact justice may be administered to all, we ask that all
disqualifications on account of race or color, so far as they apply to
voting, be removed and that the plaintiffs and defendants in every action,

whether white or black, shall be made competent witnesses with the right to testify in their own behalf, subject only to such exceptions as are made for white men. For this act of justice to our poor and oppressed race we appeal to you by every consideration of love and right. And for your favorable action will pray God's blessing upon your deliberations.

The Finance Committee reported the receipt of $125 80 to pay the expenses of the convention and the publication of its proceedings. Rev. Q. A. Graham made a very interesting and intelligent address, cautioning the delegates when they returned home that they must not think their work finished; that the world had its eyes upon them and they should keep their eyes open. After Mr. Graham's address the convention adjourned.

During the war, the soldiers being numerous in this part of the country, and my son Elisha living at a place where the soldiers frequently visited, by some cause Elisha was missed from home. The people with whom he lived treated him very bad. When the war closed I began to make inquiry for him. After many days and nights of sorrow for my boy I opened correspondence with Elder Ward Clay, of Xenia, O. Mr. Clay searched until he found him. When he had found him he wrote me the following letter:

XENIA, O., May 19, 1866.

Elder Elisha Green, Maysville, Ky, Dear Sir: At your request I have made inquiry for your boy. By having notices read in the churches and schools I have succeeded in finding him. He is six miles from Columbus, O. His fare from there to Cincinnati will be $4. If he is under twelve years of age it will be $3 50. As to my services in finding him, whatever you think is right will be satisfactory to me over and above my traveling expenses, which are $3 40. The boy will take the first train that is convenient for him, and at Cincinnati the boat *Magnolia.* I cannot say whether he will come this week or next. When he arrives you can express the money to me, as I will not be in Kentucky for two or three weeks. Send the money to David Green by express to Xenia, O. The reason of my not coming sooner is that I have a contract to put up a church in Urbana, O., which will take about four weeks. As soon as it is done I will be over. Write me on receipt of this, addressing me at Urbana, that I may know that you received it. My respects to the brethren and friends in general.

Very respectfully yours, &c., EDWARD CLAY.

According to a resolution passed in the General Association, proposing that the state be organized into District Associations, the Baptist Churches of Maysville, Mayslick and Washington sent delegates in order to be organized into what was afterwards known as the "Mt.

Zion District Association." The delegates assembled in Bethel Baptist Church, Maysville, in the year 1869. It numbered at that time only three churches, viz.: Maysville, Mayslick and Washington. The body resolved itself into a permanent organization, with me as its Moderator, R. W. T. James, Recording Secretary; L. C. Natas, Corresponding Secretary; Brother William Smith, Treasurer. Rev. R. W. T. James wrote the constitution. This session was a very good one, though nothing much done. At the second session, in 1870, at Mayslick, Ky., the following churches were represented, with delegates as follows: Baptist Church, of Maysville—Rev. E. W. Green, L. D. Henderson, William Smith, A. Stewart, H. Lee, J. A. Taylor and D. Morrison; Baptist Church, of Mayslick—Rev. L. C. Natas, William Newton, I. Parker, H. Jackson, J. H. Davis, J. Griffith, S. L. Breckinridge, Charles Hawkins and J. Middleton; Baptist Church, of Washington— H. Gibbs. H. Barnes, C. Anderson and A. Lawson. I called the meeting to order, read and sang and offered prayer. A Committee on Credentials of members was appointed; also a Committee on Permanent Organization. The following officers were elected: Rev. E. W. Green, Moderator; Rev. L. C. Natas, Recording Secretary; Charles Gray, Corresponding Secretary; Henry Jackson, Treasurer.

At 8 o'clock p. m., by appointment of the previous year, I preached the introductory sermon from Acts v:29—"We ought to obey God rather than man." Thus passed another pleasant session of the Mt. Zion District Association. The next annual session of this body was held with the Baptist Church of Washington. By this time another church was added to our list, making four, viz.: the Baptist Church of Sharpsburg, Ky. The same officers were re-elected, excepting Corresponding Secretary and Treasurer. By appointment of the session Rev. S. Jones, of Ohio, delivered the introductory sermon from Second Timothy, ii:19-20. Subject: "Baptist doctrines from the Bible." The fourth annual session of this body met with the Bethel Baptist Church, of Maysville. By this time four new churches were added to the list, viz.: Paris, Cynthiana, Scott's Station and Covington. I called the Association to order and conducted devotional exercises. Rev. John Johnson, of Cynthiana, led in prayer. The same officers were re-elected excepting Corresponding Secretary and Treasurer. Brother L. D. Henderson was elected Corresponding Secretary; Brother William Smith, Treasurer. By appointment of the body Rev. John Johnson, of Cynthiana, preached the introductory sermon from Eph. iv:5—"One Lord, One Faith, One Baptism." I was appointed as Corresponding

Messenger to General Association, which met in Georgetown the following August. It is not my intention to write a history of Mt. Zion District Association, but to mention those things so far as I am related to them. This Association continued in this way eleven years, until it became strong and influential in eastern Kentucky, and then it consolidated with the Elkhorn Association, of which I shall speak further on.

While in Paris one morning I was requested by Elder Fisher, of the M. E. Church, of Paris, to go with him to the Christian Church; that he and Rev. Ayers anticipated a discussion between themselves. Being instructed so, I went. When the time came for the discussion Elder Fisher was not present. Brother Garrett Lamb was with me. Elder Ayers in his conversation said that "the Baptists believe in the 'mourners' bench,' and they have no scripture for it. They quote the fifth chapter of Matthew to sustain them. But then Christ was addressing none but his disciples." I told him he could not prove the assertion true; that the Scriptures plainly said: "Seeing the multitude, he went up into the mountain, and when he was set, his disciples came unto him; and he taught them saying." In the conversation that passed between us there were many things said. Elder Ayers said that there was no promise of salvation this side of baptism. In refutation of that assertion, I pointed him to tenth chapter of Acts, where Cornelius received the "Gift of the Holy Ghost" while Peter was talking to him. Then the congregation was dismissed. When I came home I wrote a number of pamphlets, after this style, headed: "To the Public."

"I appear before the public in regard to a religious controversy which took place November 11, 1871, at the Christian Church in Paris. Ky., between Elder H. M. Ayers and myself. I had no idea of the discussion until I reached the church. I have thought it my duty to let the public know something about it, as I believe his object was to kill me off, but he waked up the wrong passenger. If Mr. Ayers wished a discussion why did he not do as I would have done? I would have invited him to my room. But I suppose he did not consider me worthy, and therefore he thought he would kill me off in the Christian Church. But he did not do it. Now, not that I have any unkind feeling toward Mr. Ayers, but I will point him not to the New Testament only, but to the Old. I will call the attention of the public to the word of God. Mr. Ayers asked me a question, and that was if I believed that a man was baptized for the 'remission of sins.' I asked him if I understood him to say that sins were washed away in baptism. I told him that I did not. And I shall give him a few passages of Scripture. Acts xvi:29: 'Then he called for a light and sprang in and came trembling, and fell down before Paul and Silas.' But Paul and Silas did not tell him as Mr. Ayers; 'not to do that for that was the way that the

Baptists do, and he must not do it; he must get up, it will not do to mourn that way.' As Mr. Ayers said, I want you all to read the Bible. In Acts xix:6 you will find: 'When Paul had laid his hands upon them the Holy Ghost came on them and they spake with tongues and prophesied.' But Paul did not baptize them with water. The apostles did not baptize them over again to receive the Holy Spirit. Peter tells us 'that He (God) put no difference between us and them, purifying their hearts by faith.' Now, I wish Mr. Ayers would do like them, and I think he and I would get along better. The Bible says 'if thy brother shall trespass against thee, go and tell him his fault between thee and him alone.' But Mr. Ayers reads backwards. He brought it before the church first. Now I shall ask him one question: 'Was Jesus baptized over?' I think not. If Jesus were baptized over, Paul did not do it and our Heavenly Father acknowledges John's baptism. But Mr. Ayers will not. I hope Mr. Ayers will read the Bible. Read, if you please, the fourth chapter of John. I hope Mr. Ayers is not a Pharisee. For 'When, therefore, the Lord knew how the Pharisees had heard that Jesus made and baptized more disciples than John.' Here it is said he made disciples. Will Mr. Ayers tell us how he made them? And now I point you to some chapters in the Bible which I want you to read. They are these: 'This is my blood of the new testament, which I shed for many for the remission of sins.' Read the twentieth chapter of John and the twenty-second verse and you will not see any water there. The Bible says 'the blood of Jesus and not the water.' I have not called on any of my white brethren to assist me in this. But should I, they would. I heard an elder once say that if a man fooled you the first time it was his fault and the next time it was your own fault. Elder Ayers will never fool me again in his church. May this brief epistle find its way to the hearts of many is the prayer of your unworthy servant,   E. W. GREEN."

Sometime after this controversy with Elder Ayers the Rev. E. W. Hammond, pastor of the M. E. Church of Paris, protracted a meeting in which there were well nigh 400 added to the church. Many of these desiring to be immersed or baptized, the church had a pool dug. Rev. Hammond baptized some and others he sprinkled. The following Sunday I preached in my church at Paris. In the process of which I said that baptism by immersion had planted a battery at the M. E. Church. I said this because the Rev. Hammond had said there were seven ways to baptize. Mr. Hammond was editing a small paper called the *District Monitor*. When I came home I was shown the following item in his paper:

There is quite an extensive movement on the part of the younger and more progressive members of the Baptist Church in Paris in favor of a change of pastors. They want an educated minister. We hope their wants may be gratified. Paris needs more light.

There was no truth in that item. The young members of Paris church had said no such thing. On my return to Paris, at my next regular appointment, I was in company with Brother Henry Crosse, an intimate friend of mine and a member of Rev. Hammond's church, and who has since died. I told Brother Crosse that Rev. Hammond had published me in his paper. He said that he thought not. I contended that it was so, when the Rev. Mr. Hammond comes up. Brother Crosse asked him if he said anything concerning me in his paper. He said he did publish a little something about the church of which I was pastor. Then I told him that what he had published was not true, and that he must correct it. If he did not I would. I came home and waited nearly a month for Mr. Hammond to correct the statement which he had made. I then wrote the following:

Once more I appear before the public for the purpose of correcting some false statements that the Rev. E. W. Hammond, editor of the *District Monitor*, has made. I will tell him the truth. I will write just what he put into his little fly-trap. He might have known that he could not catch a fool in that, for the Bible says we must become fools in order to be made wise. So I say to the editor, E. W. Hammond. He said: "There is quite an extensive movement on the part of the younger and more progressive members of the Baptist Church in Paris in favor of a change of pastors. They want an educated minister. We hope their wishes may be gratified. Paris needs more light." Well, while we know that is true, the editor takes it on himself to say that for the Baptist Church in Paris. The church in Paris has never said that. And so, Elder, you are not a Bishop over the Baptist Church in Paris; and if you are I shall wait until our General Association meets and if our head Bishop, G. W. Dupee, has put you over me, I shall take him down. You have just as much as you can do well. There are some men that have a little learning and they are so afraid that the people won't know it that they have to keep meddling with other people's business. I reckon you think that I have been in Paris long enough. But you are not the judge. I am thankful that church and state are not together; for if they were you would put me into your "fly-trap" and kill me. But, Elder, I am still in my fort and I hope you will let me stay in Paris this year, if you please. I will try and be a good boy and will promise to say just what I please, for I am in my fort, and when I am not there I have a body-guard to watch while I am trying to preach the gospel. God has promised to be with me while I am trying to preach the gospel and I shall not mind E. W. H. But I think you treated me bad, for I think that all ministers have just as much as they can do to attend to their own business. I want to say to you, Elder, that you have as many ministers that need education as the Baptists. I think you had better look at home for them and put them into your little "fly-trap." I think you had better look at home first and when you get through come and preach for me a good gospel sermon for you owe me one. You say: "Paris needs more light." Well, that is true. But if you mean false light, I think Paris has enough of that light and do not think it advisable for the Elder to waste his paper with a fool and that kind of light. If you cannot find any truth outside of the Bible I would advise you to look inside of it, and there is as much as you need. You gave my church in Paris a pretty heavy stroke with your little "fly-trap." Don't you know that Christ said "Blessed are the peace-makers, for they shall be called the children of God?" You are a young man and I think you would do well to preach the gospel and let others alone.

And now I will say something about myself. Last winter, when I was baptizing in Paris, I said that "Baptism by immersion had planted a battery at the M. E. Church." If I did not tell the truth I would like to know what it is. You said you did not want it for sprinkling or pouring, and that there were seven ways to baptize. Well I had just as soon you had said there were a hundred. If you are editor of a political paper I must reconsider the matter, and if a Christian paper I think you ought to go to the Bible for truth. You say that you are an old-fashioned Methodist—a real live member of the church. For fear that the Elder may think, like my other friend, that is, that I did not write this, I will be good enough to tell him how I learnt to write. My young mistress taught me to write when I was a slave. Her name was Miss Alice Dobbyns. But it never forced me off the track. You don't think the colored people of Paris and the south have any sense, because they have never been to college. Why, Elder, I did not know that all the books were in college. Brother Isaac Williams, who is a gentleman and a Christian, has a book which if you will read, you will find that you are not so old as you think. I will tell you what page to look on—the sixtieth. You will find that John Wesley was educated for the ministry and took orders as a priest in the Episcopal Church of England while he was still a young man. He arrived in the Savannah river in the year of our Lord 1736 and he was not converted then. You must read history and then you will not be so old as you think you are. And now let me tell you something as a friend. The next man you put into your "fly-trap" you find out where he was raised. But if you can't find anybody but E. W. Green put him in and say what you please about him; you can't make matters any worse. You are free and so am I. You know a fool won't work. You think I have no sense and you will not mind me. As it is wrong to beat a fool, I hope you will let me stay in Paris this year. The Baptists in Paris want me this year. But you want the Baptist Church in Paris to have an educated man. Now, Elder, that will do to tell some people, but it will not do to tell sensible folks. You might get hurt, dear brother. Stop, if you please. You might run afoul of some man and get hurt, but not me. I have no education. You promised Brother Henry Crosse and me that you would correct the item in your paper and that you would send me a copy, and you have not done it. I told you if you did not I would. I never would tell falsehoods when I was a slave and I will not now. I have always found it as much as I can do to keep my own house clean. And now, I bring my letter to a close. Yours in Christ, E. W. GREEN.

The Rev. E. W. Hammond is a fine educated man, but he lacked something. He wrote too quick without close thought. Had he studied a proposition closely, weighed matters candidly in his mind; studied the disadvantages of slavery and its oppositions through which the old ministers had come, he would not have put such an item in his paper denouncing me as an ignorant preacher. But after this we got along very well. If it were not that I am writing my own history I would not mention it at all. But as it makes an important item in my life, being somewhat connected with it, I do not withhold it from these pages. Should the Rev. Mr. Hammond any time after I am dead read these lines, he will only laugh and express himself surprisingly at this being in history. He will say that he never, when in Paris in charge of the M. E. Church, editing a paper, thought once the item written by him, touching the Baptist Church and pastor, would be an item of history. I will just say, that while in Covington two months ago, attending the Association, I met Rev. Hammond. We expressed ourselves joyfully of the past. He is in charge of the large M. E. Church, Ninth street, Covington.

In May of 1875 I went to Louisville as a delegate from here to the State Republican Convention. The object of the convention was to nominate state officers. When business of the convention was finished I came to Paris and staid there till the train left for Maysville. I boarded the train at Paris for home. I was sitting at the extreme end behind and so was Rev. Preston Taylor, of the Christian Church. When we got to Millersburg the bridge gave way, the coupling pin broke and the car that we were in fell back, one end on the bridge and the other on the abutment. It was so steep that a person could scarcely walk up it. I never knew when my leg was broke. When I discovered that it was broken one foot was about four inches in the water. On the opposite side sat a Methodist preacher who came and pulled my leg from under the stove. By this time I had discovered that my leg was broken. I lifted my right leg out of the water and tried the left, but it appeared as heavy as if there were a log attached to it. At this time Mrs. Herrick and daughter were sitting in the car before me. Her ankle was fastened and she was pulling and screaming, i. e., Mrs. Herrick. I told her that she had better stop; that if her ankle was not broken she might break it. I then looked over on the opposite side and old Mr. Sharp was lying flat on his back with the seats on top of him. He was throwing them up and they in turn falling back. I spoke to him and told him that he was making it worse and he stopped at once. I thought that he was dead. Before I left Millersburg he came and I told him of it, and he could not recollect it. The conductor hearing me talk to Mrs. Herrick and Mr. Sharp told me to get up and come out. I told him I could not for my leg was broken. He asked me how I knew. I told him that I was holding it together. They rushed to me to take me out. They came much excited. I told them to stop. They stopped. I told them to take the broken leg and put over the good one. A white gentleman took hold of the leg just where it was broke, and they carried me up to Marshall Wheeler's, for Sister Wheeler had said that she wanted me brought to her house. They laid me on the bed until the doctors got ready to set it. There were seven doctors. They all said that they were going to help set my leg. From the shock that I had received from the fall I was very cold. The doctors sent some one out to get some whisky. In a short time they came with it. A glass of it was sweetened and brought to me. I told them that I did not want it; that when I died I wanted to die sober, not drunk. I had on a new pair of boots. They said that in order to get them off they must cut them. I told them not to cut those boots. They wanted to know then how to get them off. I told them to raise me up. I held the broken leg until they pulled it off. The brethren at Paris hearing of my misfortune sent Brother Garrett Lamb to wait on me. Brother Lamb did so like a true Christian gentleman. He deserves the credit of the church that sent him, the blessing of God and all I can do for him while he lives. While I was in Millersburg the citizens of Maysville made up $37 and gave it to Lawyer Wadsworth, requesting him to pay me a visit and give it to me. Mr. Wadsworth did so. I never shall forget the citizens of Maysville and Millersburg and other places for their kindness to me when in that condition. They all attended to me and brought nourishment of all descriptions.

In the meantime my wife, who is now resting under the sod, waiting the sound of the trump of God, came to see me. She rode all night. When she got to the door in the morning I saw that she was greatly troubled. I told her not to cry, that I was not dead. Then she smiled and came in. Had I staid in Millersburg until the coming Friday I would have been there six weeks.

While I was sick the Superintendent of the road and all the company came to see me. They told me that whatever I wanted to ask for it. After I came home the President of the road and his wife continued to visit me. When I got nearly well he came and asked what would I take to compromise and not bring suit against the company. He said that Mr. Taylor had compromised for $500. Well, as they had been so good to me and as I had my hands in their pocket, I thought to leave them some money, so I compromised for the same as Mr. Taylor. Mrs. Herrick sued them for $5,000. She was successful in it. I started on my crutches to the depot. When I got there the train had gotten over the trestle work a short distance from the depot. When they saw me they came back. I mention this to show the feeling they had for me. While I was sick the church at Paris secured the services of the Rev. John Johnson, of Cynthiana, and the Rev. J. W. Calamese, of Paris. I was preaching in about two months after I was hurt.

The following year after the accident at Millersburg, and in February of that year, the Baptist cause was shocked by the death of one of its faithful veterans, the Rev. R. Lee, pastor of the Baptist Church of Georgetown, Ky. The Rev. Messrs. Lee and Dupee and myself were intimate friends. Before his death, and during his illness, I visited him and staid some considerable time. This noble minister of Jesus Christ departed this life on the 26th of February, 1876. When the day came for the funeral the church was packed and all out of doors was thronged with people to hear the last words in due respect to the body of that noble Christian minister. The Rev. J. F. Thomas, another eye witness, wrote the following to the *Baptist Herald*, the Baptist organ edited by the Rev. G. W. Dupee, of Paducah:

GEORGETOWN, KY., February 27, 1876.

The funeral of Elder R. Lee, pastor of the Colored Baptist Church, Georgetown, who departed this life February 23, 1876, at 6 o'clock a. m., was largely attended by a vast concourse of people. The corpse was taken to the church at 10 o'clock a. m. for review by the assembled congregation, and at 12 the coffin was closed and services commenced. The Rev. J. F. Thomas, of Lexington, read the twenty-third Psalm. The Rev. R. Martin, of Frankfort, offered prayer. The Rev. M. M. Bell, of Lexington, read and sang the 1118th hymn—"Servant of God, Well Done" &c. After singing the above hymn Elder George W. Dupee, of Paducah, gave a synopsis of the life and labors of Bishop Lee, stating that he had been engaged, if the longest liver, for twenty-five or thirty years to preach the funeral of Brother Lee. He first met the deceased near the Big Springs in the fall of 1845—thirty years ago this fall. Bishop Lee was born July 25, 1825; died February 23, 1876, aged fifty years, five months and twenty-three days. He embraced religion when young and joined the Presbyterian Society in 1842 and remained with it until 1862, when he was baptized in the fellowship of

Pleasant Green Baptist Church, Lexington, by Elder G. W. Dupee. He was ordained August 7, 1862, by Elders W. Pratt, J. S. Smith and G. W. Dupee, and was called to pastor the Second Baptist Church in Georgetown in the fall of the same year. His labors there were very successful. He baptized into the fellowship of this church 975 persons in fourteen years. Having been called to divide his labors with the Second Baptist Church of Versailles he entered upon such duty the first Lord's day in January, 1864, where his labors met with like success. But a few weeks before his death he resigned his pastorate with that church, having baptized 619 persons. Total number baptized for the two churches, 1,594. Brother Dupee promised to give a full report of the labors of Bishop Lee in the April number of the *Baptist Herald.*

The speaker read for his text 2d Timothy, iv:7-8. We cannot give a detail of sermon, but we will say this much: the speaker displayed the power of oratory that he is well known to possess. He said: "Thirty years ago Reuben Lee, the slave of old Mr. Samuel Wallace, heard that form of doctrine which was delivered and obeyed it from the heart. It was not his fault that he did not at first join the church of Jesus Christ, but being a slave he had to join the Presbyterian Society. But as soon as he got possession of himself he joined the Pleasant Green Baptist Church in 1862 and entered upon the work of a minister of the gospel."

At the conclusion of Elder Dupee's discourse Elder H. McDonald, pastor of the white church, was invited by Elder Dupee to make some remarks, which he did with a feeling eloquence characteristic of the man.

Elder E. W. Green was the last speaker. He adverted to his first acquaintance with Brother Lee and of the pleasantness he had with him. He filled up and took his seat.

Thousands of people, white and colored, followed the remains to the grave. When the benediction was pronounced the multitude dispersed until the great day. May we all be ready.   J. F. THOMAS.

The Rev. G. W. Dupee in the same issue of the *Herald* said: "Here the members and friends had prepared the church suitably, it being heavily draped. A fine metallic coffin and everything showed their intelligence and also the great respect they entertained for their lamented pastor. The ministering brethren were generally invited, we understood. The following named bishops were present, to-wit: E. W. Green, R. Martin, L. C. Natas, J. Johnson, J. F. Thomas, M. M. Bell, C. Smothers, J. K. Polk, L. Burley, M. Madison, P. Vinegar, D. Hickman, S. Lee, N. Williams, J. Jackson, L. Lewis and H. McDonald, pastor of the white church. A number of students from Georgetown College, members of the churches of Versailles, Lexington, Paris, Frankfort, Midway and from various churches about through the country. The scene was truly appalling. His last words in the pulpit, just fifty-seven hours before he died, were that he knew that he had been born of the spirit of God—that Paul had two sons in the gospel,

Timothy and Titus—so have I (alluding to J. K. Polk and John Vinegar.)"

I need add no more to this sublime and solemn scene, but close it by saying that the Rev. Lee was in every way an example for the believers. He was a true gospel minister in action, soul and purpose of heart. I can say that the Baptists of Kentucky have lost a faithful minister in the work of the Master. Would that our ministry of to-day was such—that the same earnest zeal for the salvation of men and the progress of God's cause could be found in our younger ministers of the present age.

The Elkhorn Association got into a kind of tangle and could not pay for their minutes. They sent a committee to the Mt. Zion District Association, asking if we would consolidate with them. The Association set a time to consider the matter. The time came and the meeting was held in the Baptist Church at Paris. The Executive Boards of both bodies were the authorities in the matter.

PARIS, KY., July 30, 1879.

At a joint meeting of the Executive Boards of Mt. Zion and Elkhorn District Associations, convened in High Street Baptist Church, credentials from their Associations authorizing them to consolidate the two bodies, were produced. The devotional exercises were conducted by Elder E. W. Green, after which he was elected Moderator and Brother E. M. Manion Secretary. On motion it was order d that a committee be appointed to draft resolutions favoring consolidation. The committee produced the following preamble and resolutions:

"WHEREAS, the several district associations in this section of the state are becoming weak, be it

"*Resolved*. That the Elkhorn and Mt. Zion District Associations be consolidated and that this body be known hereafter as the Consolidated Baptist Educational Association; that the Constitution of the Mt. Zion be recognized as the Constitution of the Consolidated Baptist Educational Association.

"*Resolved*, That the Consolidated Baptist Educational Association meet at Covington, Ky., Wednesday before the third Lord's day in July, 1880. We further recommend that some steps be taken to establish a school at Scott's Station, or elsewhere in Kentucky, and that the Executive Board of the Consolidated Baptist Educational Association be the committee to carry out the resolution.

"*Resolved*, That the Rev. E. W. Green be Moderator of the Consolidated Baptist Educational Association; J. Johnson, Assistant Moderator; J. W. Calamese, Recording Secretary; L. D. Henderson, Corresponding Secretary; William Smith, Treasurer.

J. F. THOMAS,
E. W. GREEN,
C. SMOTHERS,
J. K. POLK, } Committee.
W. B. BLACKBURN,
J. JOHNSON,

The Rev. W. B. Blackburn was one of the most energetic and active men in the business of the Association. I could take him and do as much business as some six men. At the meeting of the Consolidated Baptist Educational Association with the Baptist Church of Covington, it was shocked by the absence of the Rev. W. B. Blackburn, the pastor in charge, who had died the April previous. The following resolutions in respect to his death were adopted:

WHEREAS, God, in His allwise providence, has moved from the world our much beloved and revered brother, Bishop W. B. Blackburn, of Covington, and

WHEREAS, This, the Consolidated Baptist Educational Association of which he was a member, while bowing in submission to the will of God, misses him in her deliberations; and

WHEREAS, The loss of our brother in the vineyard of the Lord has caused us to grieve much, therefore be it

Resolved, That through his demise we have lost an earnest soldier of the cross, an eloquent expounder of the truth as it is in Jesus Christ, an able defender of the doctrine of the Baptist Church, a man whose heart was ever ready to assist the poor, raise the fallen, cheer the faint, and in whom was personification of all that is true. Be it further

Resolved, That our association wear the usual badge of mourning and that we cast the mantle of charity over his faults, be they few or many, and think only of his virtue, feeling assured that he passed over the river to welcome us across. Be it further

Resolved, That these resolutions be published in the several city papers and a copy sent to his mother and family; that we condole his bereft mother and bid her await with patience the time when she will be permitted to join him on the other shore "where the wicked cease from troubling and the weary are at rest." Be it further

Resolved, That each church in the bounds of this Association hold a memorial service in favor of him and that to-morrow afternoon it be held in this Association.

W. J. Simmons, D.D., J. K. Polk, J. L. Dudley, Brothers L. D. Henderson, O. A. Nelson, W. M. Ward composed the committee for the above resolutions. Accordingly, Sunday at the afternoon session, the Association and citizens of Covington and Cincinnati assembled in the First Baptist Church to participate in his memorial service. It was a grand, solemn and large gathering. When the Rev. J. L. Dudley had announced those who were to participate in the services, the Rev. J. K. Polk sang the hymn "Servant of God well done." The Rev. J. W. Calamese offered prayer. I opened the services, choosing for a text Job xiv:14— "If a man die shall he live again?" I was followed by the Rev. Messrs. J. K. Polk. J. Johnson, J. W. Calamese and William Miller. Thus passed another scene of solemnity in the Baptist Church in Covington.

CHAPTER VI.

IN September of 1880 I received a dispatch from Maysville to come at once, that my wife was "spitting blood" and was not expected to live. I left Paris at once for home. It was the Lord's will and I got there a short time before she died. I conversed with her concerning her prospects for heaven and speaking of the goodness of God. Said she, in substance: "My time is at hand, and all is well." While it was upon me a heavy stroke of sorrow, yet I bowed in humble submission to the will of God that in His providence He was doing all things well in separating us. Finally she fell asleep in Christ. The following article concerning her death was printed in one of the city papers:

"Sister Susan Green, wife of our venerable father in the gospel. Elder E. W. Green, of Maysville, departed this life September 13. 1880. She professed religion fifty years ago and received the ordinance of baptism at the hands of the Rev. Walter Warder. Thirty-five years ago she was married to Elder Green and together they lived happily for that long space of time. Sister Green's life was not an uneventful one. She suffered much, both physically and mentally. She was born a slave, and after marrying was at one time compelled to witness that most dreadful of all sights—the carrying away of her own child (a son) to the slave markets of the south. The little fellow was tied to a stake barefooted and almost naked in winter. She bade him a tearful adieu, her heart bleeding and yearning for her child which the accursed yoke of slavery prevented her from claiming as her own and whom she never saw again. Surely the Lord loved her for he has chastened her. She meekly said 'Thy willl be done.' Some two years ago the Lord laid his hand upon her again. This time she received a paralytic stroke. which disabled her for awhile. A few weeks ago she was able to stand alone, for the first time since she was stricken. A few days ago she was confined to her bed by her last illness. Every possible remedy was used and all were unremitting in their attentions to her wants, but in spite of all that was done she continued to sink. Shortly before her death, feeling the hour was nigh, when her desire to be with Christ would be gratified, she called her niece, Sister Nelson, to her side and told her the hymns which she desired to be sung at her funeral, viz: 'On Jordan's stormy banks I stand,' 'Come brothers and sisters that love one another.' She bade all farewell and sank to sleep in the arms of Jesus and awoke in that happy place 'where the wicked cease from troubling and the weary are at rest.' Her funeral services were conducted by Elders John Johnson, of Cynthiana; James Thomas, of Paris, and J. W. Calamese, of Washington. Elder Johnson's text was First Corinthians, xv:55—'O death, where is thy sting? O grave, where is thy victory?' It was an able discourse. He was followed by Elders Thomas and Calamese with very appropriate remarks. At the conclusion of the services the remains were carried to their last resting place, followed by a large concourse of people. Surely a mother in Israel has gone and we can only wait for our time to cross to meet her where parting is no more. She has left a husband and children to mourn her loss, but that dear husband is not as one without hope, for he looks forward to the time when he can meet her on the banks of sweet deliverance. We who knew her but a short while can add our testimony and say with the inspired writer: 'Blessed are the dead who die in the Lord, yet from henceforth saith the spirit for they may rest from their labors and their works do follow them.' "

The writer of this article was D. L. V. Moffett, to whom I give due credit for the manner and spirit thereof. Not long after the death of my wife my daughter Maria was stricken very severely, which resulted in her losing her mind and thus having to be taken to the Lexington Asylum, where she died in a short time. In the Cincinnati riot of April, 1884, my son Thomas was killed by some misfortune, what it was I am unable to say.

On the 8th of June, 1883, I left home for Paris, the following Sunday of course being my regular day there. When I got to Millersburg the train was boarded by the Rev. G. T. Gould, President of the Millersburg Female College, Professors Bristow and Carrington, connected with the same institution, and a number of lady students from the college. Colonel Morrow, an intimate friend of mine, rose up politely and said to Gould: "You may have my seat." "No," said he. "I'll make this nigger get up." When he said this he and Professor

Bristow took hold of me with the expression: "Come out of here."

I said to them: "I paid for this seat in Maysville. I will hold it to Paris or die in my tracks."

"Then you won't come out?"

I told him "No; that if he had asked me like a gentleman I would have come out, but before I would be pulled out like a dog I would die." He then asked:

"Did you call me no gentleman?"

Said I: "No sir; had you asked me like a gentleman I would have got up."

The Rev. John Barbour, who is a gentleman and Christian, when I got to Paris came to me and asked if I were going to let that ghost off. I told him that I was not. "Well," said he, "if you want my testimony you can get it, for I saw it all." Bristow came up to Mr. Barbour and said to him:

"Do you take this old scoundrel's part? If you do, I will give you what the nigger got."

Mr. Barbour told him that he was traveling, and desired to keep out of difficulties with any one.

I got off the train and went down in town, (Paris,) when Mr. Charlton Alexander came hunting me. When he met me, said he: "You were in a fuss on the train this evening." I told him that I was. Continued he: "What are you going to do about it?" I told him that I thought that I would go home and consult with my friends. He said: "No; you have friends here. Go up to Mr. Lockhart's and get out a warrant for 'assault and battery.'" He went with me and I did so. He told me to go down to the lower livery stable and that I would find Colonel Morrow, who knew all the party, and if he were not at the stable to go to his house. I did as instructed. The Colonel had just left for home. I went to his house and was invited in and given a seat. He asked me if I knew the party. I told him that I did not. "Well," said he, "I know them all." He gave me a number of names, stating that on the morrow he was going to Millersburg and would return on the evening train and present to me the balance. It was such a peculiar affair that I must give the opinion of Gould, Bristow and the press generally. Let us hear the statement of Mr. Gould in the Maysville *Bulletin*

Mr. Editor: Commencement duties have prevented me heretofore from noticing the many misrepresentations of my encounter with Rev.

Elisha Green, a man of color, upon the Maysville and Lexington train, June 8, 1883. At the time referred to I had twenty-eight young ladies under my care. Attention to the baggage detained me so that I was the very last to board the train, doing so only after it was pretty well under headway. As soon as I entered the ladies' coach I noticed considerable excitement and heard such exclamations as "It is a shame" "He ought to be put out!" "If he does not get up he ought to be made to." The matter was explained when I saw from the rear door two of my young ladies standing in the aisle and a big black negro man complacently occupying a seat to himself. I looked and there was not a vacant seat in the car except the one beside the negro. In many places the young ladies were sitting three upon a seat and several gentlemen were standing in the passway, having given up their places. Among them standing were Professors Bristow, Carrington, Payne, McClintock, Waddel and Piper and my own son. As the two young ladies had already been standing some moments directly at the end of the seat on which the negro sat it was evident that he had no intention of offering them the place. I therefore walked back to him and said to him: "I wish you would give your seat to these young ladies, because if you do not there will be a disturbance." He promptly replied that he would not. "Very well," said I, "when the conductor comes we will see whether you do not." I then sent for Captain Martin, who was in the front coach, and waited no little time for his coming, since he did not come directly, but stopped to take up all the tickets by the way. While I was thus waiting and the young ladies still standing the negro informed me that if the conductor compelled him to give them his seat he would make the railroad company suffer for it. When Conductor Martin at last reached us I appealed to him whether the young ladies must stand and let the negro sit. His reply was that he could do nothing. "All right," said I, "then I will see what I can do." Leaning over the back of the seat I took the negro by the arm, saying: "Come, get out of here." At once, and with considerable violence, he struck me and loosened my grasp. Then it was that Professor Bristow, who was sitting on the arm of the second seat in front of us, and who had neither spoken to the darkey nor been at any time near him, seeing him viciously strike me, rose up and struck the fellow over the head with a small hand bag. Professor Bristow hit him but once and Mr. Carrington never touched him at all in any way, manner, shape or form. Nor did I touch his person other than to take him by the arm as already described. I did not know who the fellow was. I did know, however, that he was a big black negro and that two young ladies were standing while he sat. Having never been accustomed to see such an indignity as that put upon a lady, that she must stand through a ride of eight miles while a negro man lolls at his ease, I could not bring myself tamely to submit to it. I do not believe that there is a gentleman in Kentucky who would stand idly by and see his wife and daughters thus insulted. These young ladies came from the extreme south, hundreds of miles from their homes, with neither father nor mother near, but depending upon me for protection from insult and injury. I had been recreant to my trust and unworthy the position which I occupy had I not, after exhausting appeal to the negro and conductor, myself attempted his ejection from the seat. If any man has fallen so low as to think white women should stand while negro men keep their seats then him I have insulted, and really I do not care if I have.   Yours, &c.,

                                                    GEO. T. GOULD.

Millersburg Female College, June 19, 1883.

Here Mr. Gould's statement ends. I take the liberty to say that there is not an ounce of truth in the thing. I am a negro, as Mr. Gould says, but I would rather be a big black negro with the character and reputation I have. and one that tells the truth, than an educated dude of a white man that can lie faster than the Recording Angel in heaven would have patience to write. There is an expression which says: "A lie can go a mile while truth is putting his boots on."

Let us turn to another statement of the affair by one of Mr. Gould's colleagues—Professor Bristow. The *Daily Bulletin* of Thursday, June 21, 1883, contained the following:

The following explanation of the assault on the Rev. Elisha Green, of this city, is printed in the Paris *Kentuckian* as coming from Professor Bristow:

"Meeting Professor Bristow, of the Millersburg Female College, and a pleasant party of young ladies on Saturday's train, we asked him to record the names in our note book, which he did as follows: Professor F. L. Bristow, Tuscaloosa, Ala.; Miss Jennie Sanders, Parksburg. West Va. 'All seated and no Rev. African molested,' added he. We then asked him as to the facts of the case in regard to the difficulty with the colored man Green. 'As we went into the car,' said he, 'several persons made way to let the young ladies have seats and we expected the darkey to do likewise, and after waiting sometime asked him if he did not intend to take another seat and let the ladies have his. He was positive that he would not do so. We waited for the conductor to make Green act the part of a gentleman, but the conductor did not feel authorized to interfere with him, and we said that we would force him to act the part of a gentleman. Mr. Gould attempted to draw him out of the seat when Green struck at him, and I tapped the darkey with this light satchel. I knew nothing of his being a preacher or crippled, as he is a very large, robust-looking darkey, and I notice gets about very well. I think any man, white or black, that won't readily accommodate ladies, ought be made to do so. I knocked a darkey down once in Little Rock, Ark., who would not give way to ladies in the street. I did tell a man, (said to be the Rev. John Barbour) who sided with Green, that I could accommodate him.'"

This ends the statement of Professor Bristow. I made a statement in the beginning of the case, but I wish to make the one that I wrote to

the paper when the act was committed, because it was then fresh in my memory.· I wrote to the *Bulletin*, of this city, by request, as follows:

On Friday, the 8th day of June, having occasion to go to Paris, where I have a charge in connection with the Maysville church, I bought a ticket to that place and occupied a seat on one of the cars of the 12:30 p. m. train until I got to Millersburg. At that place a man, whom I afterwards learned was Dr. G. T. Gould, of the Female Institute at Millersburg, with several other men and a number of young ladies, came into the car and for several minutes were busy seating seating themselves. I paid no particular attention to them as there were vacant enough seats for all, and presently all were seated except two ladies. Colonel Robert Morrow, who occupied the seat immediately behind me, arose and offered it to them. But one of the teachers, Professor Bristow, said: " No, I don't want your seat; I'll make this nigger get up." And with that he siezed me suddenly by the collar and said: "Come out of here," and at the same time Dr. Gould caught me by the arm. I told them I had paid for that seat from Maysville and did not intend to be driven out like a dog. I had no notice that it was wanted, and would have given it up if I had been asked politely, and if there had been no other seats in the car I should have offered it to them. I try to be polite on all occasions, and I do not think any person in this city who knows me will ever say that I have been intentionally impolite to any one. When I told Professor Bristow that I did not intend to be driven out of my seat he stepped into the aisle and into the second seat ahead of me and struck me three or four times over the head with a valise while Dr. Gould and some other person held me. At this point Colonel Morrow and some other gentlemen, among them Conductor John Martin, interfered and saved me from further injury. There was one cut on the top of my head and cuts on two of my fingers. At Paris, on the following Monday, I procured warrants against the men who assailed me on the charge of "assault and battery," and I shall be present at the proper time to present my case against them in court.

E. W. GREEN.

Under my article the editor penned the following: " Rev. Elisha Green is sixty-five years of age and has been a minister of the gospel for thirty-nine years, all of that time pastor of the Maysville Colored Baptist Church, and since 1855 has also had charge of the church at Paris. He is a quiet and unobtrusive man and is esteemed and respected not only by his own race, but also by the white population of Maysville. He was injured several years ago in a railroad accident and has since been a cripple."

Having given the statements of Dr. Gould, Professor Bristow and myself, I will give the opinion of the press in general. The Lexington *Transcript* of June 19, 1883, had the following:

Northern papers to the contrary, there is a deep-seated sense of justice to the black man in the breast of our best white men that arouses their indignation in this community upon a broad and catholic principle of right in which color and social condition do not at all enter. The Reverend President, G. T. Gould, of Millersburg, who struck the old black preacher, Elisha Green, has in the public estimation so proclaimed himself a bad citizen that any college or church that carries him will have to do it as Sinbad did the old man of the sea. That institution cannot flourish until that man and the other two associated with him are dismissed from its employ. Such men are not proper characters to entrust with young girls. This man Gould is the same party that Mrs. Tarrant, of our city, and other lady teachers in his school declined to be associated with, on the ground of ungentlemanly conduct in him. A mule and plow at this season would have been a more fitting situation for the development of the reverend fellow's genius and manners than one in which he is liable to be looked to as an example of decorum by our best young ladies.

Now, to affirm the statement made by the Lexington *Transcript*, I will give the following, coming from a citizen of Maysville:

When Rev. George T. Gould lived in Maysville some years ago he was well thought of by members of all denominations. But since he has been teaching the Female Seminary in Millersburg various reports prejudicial to his reputation have obtained circulation and among many persons credence. Whether the charges of intemperance have been true or false his conduct on the afternoon train last Friday in assaulting Elisha Green, the well-known colored Baptist preacher of this city, was a most unwarrantable outrage. We have only to say of Elisha Green that his character as a man, honest, truthful, peaceful, religious, is one that Mr. Gould and many other white ministers might covet. His conduct in this community, where his life as a slave and free man were passed, has been above reproach and beyond suspicion. On Friday last he paid for a passage from this city to Paris, and took the seat to which his ticket entitled him. He occupied it without molestation and without disturbing any one until he reached Millersburg, where the car was boarded by the Rev. Dr. Gould, his assistant Professor Bristow, and about thirty young ladies found seats. Gould demanded that Elisha Green should surrender the seat he occupied, which he declined to do. They appealed to Conductor Martin, who told them that Green had paid for half of the seat and had a right to keep it and he would not remove him; that if either of them desired the other half he would see that Green yielded it; that he was a respectable man, a minister of the gospel and should not be disturbed. Martin then left the car and Gould and Bristow continued their altercation with Green and finally both assaulted him, beating him over the head with satchels. If the facts be as stated to us it was a most unmanly outrage, degrading to Mr. Gould's character as a minister of the gospel, and as a teacher of youth unworthy of any one professing to be a gentleman. It was pure, unadulterated cowardly ruffianism and none guilty of it ought to be tolerated in the pulpit or as the principal of a school to which young ladies are sent to be instructed in manners and morals. A white minister of the gospel was on board of the train, who had known Green all his life, and told him he had witnessed the assault and would give his testimony if called on. Whereupon Bristow, with characteristic blackguardism and ruffianism, offered to fight him, which of course was declined.

COWARDLY ASSAULT.

Rev. E. W. Green, Colored, of This City, Assailed and Beaten—Details of the Disgraceful Affair as Given By an Eye-Witness.

A most cowardly and brutal assault was made upon Rev. Elisha Green on board the Kentucky Central Railroad train on Friday by Rev. G. T. Gould, President of the Millersburg Female College, and Professors Bristow and Carrington, connected with the same institution. Rev. Elisha Green was *en route* for Paris, where he was to preach Sunday. When the train reached Millersburg it was boarded by Rev. G. T. Gould, Professors Bristow and Carrington, and a large number of young ladies of the college on their way to Versailles, where they were to give an exhibition that night.

Conductor John Martin, in an interview with the reporter of the *New Republican*, says he was approached by Rev. Gould, who demanded of him the removal of Rev. Green from the car. He refused to do so, stating that he was an old colored preacher who had always acted gentlemanly during the frequent trips he had made on his train, and that he was entitled to one-half the seat he was occupying; that he would see that they secured the other half should they desire it. Rev. Gould responded: "If you don't put him out we will" and commenced drawing off his gloves. Conductor Martin states that he passed on collecting tickets, never thinking there would be any trouble, as all the parties were preachers, but was immediately recalled by a scuffle and loud words. When he reached the spot Professor Carrington was mounted on the seat holding Rev. Green, Rev. Gould pinioning him from behind and Professor Bristow raining blows with a brass-bound valise upon his head. He commanded Bristow to desist, who rather reluctantly consented when informed by Conductor Martin that if he did not he would compel him to do so. Conductor Martin says utmost confusion prevailed, the passengers rushing out into other cars. Colonel Robert Morrow, of Paris, in an interview with the Bourbon *News* reporter, substantially confirms Conductor Martin, and further states that he tendered his seat to Rev. Gould, who replied: "No, I thank you; I don't want that seat. I am going to have that one and he has got to get out of here." Colonel Morrow and others also state to the *News* that Professor Carrington attempted to draw a pistol, but on being admonished not to attempt it he did not do so. Another eye-witness is authority for the statement that Professor Bristow attempted to open his valise as if to get a pistol. It is further stated that on the arrival of the train at Paris Rev. John Barbour, who had witnessed the difficulty, told Green he would give his testimony if called on, whereupon Bristow, who overheard him, stepped up and informed him if he desired to have a "finger in the pie" he could be accommodated.

We have given a statement of the affair at length that the facts might be fully understood. It is apparent that it makes a strong case of double-distilled cowardly ruffianism that we would not have believed any Kentuckian would have been guilty of. The case is more brutal when it is taken in consideration that Rev. Elisha Green is advanced in years and enfeebled by an injury received on the road near the place of his assault several years ago, whilst his assailants were three strong, vigorous, able-bodied men, and one of whom could have handled him. It is a shocking and disgusting outrage when we consider that the attack was made upon a colored man, and we are of the firm belief that it never would have been attempted if he (Green) had been white. It evinces base, brutal and degraded minds which assaulted and would perhaps have gone further if they had not been restrained. It proclaims to the world that they are totally unfitted for the positions they hold as educators of the morals of young ladies. It is a disgrace they have brought upon the ministry for which they should be fittingly rebuked by the church to which they belong. Finally, it betrays the wolf in sheep's clothing—the most vicious and despicable of characters.

—[*Maysville New Republican.*

There can be no doubt but that Dr. Gould, Professor Bristow and Secretary Carrington have made a serious mistake and placed themselves in an ugly attitude before the public.   —[*Carlisle Mercury.*

Having put out a warrant on Mr. Gould for "assault and battery," as advised by Mr. Alexander, the case came up in March of the year 1884 in the Paris Courthouse. Mr. G. C. Lockhart was my employe and Mr. Harry Ward, of Cynthiana, was the attorney for Gould. The cost of the suit was $300 and the court allowed me $24 damages. I will present a synopsis of what took place in process of the trial. Mr. Ward addressed the jury in this manner:

"*Judge, Your Honor, Gentlemen of the Jury:* Here is Bishop Green, Elder Green, Rev. Green, and I believe the conductor calls him 'Uncle 'Lisha.' Don't you know that it is wrong for you to go to law? And here you sit in the Courthouse attending a law suit and I look up to you for instruction. Brother 'Lisha, you don't like to be called a negro."

Said I: "So far as nigger is concerned I do not like that; but negro, I am proud of it."

This is merely the beginning of Mr. Ward's speech. Mr. Lockhart followed.

"*Judge. Your Honor, Gentlemen of the Jury:* I am a lawyer and sworn to enforce the law. I intend to do it irrespective of race, color or previous condition of servitude. My opponent, all he has done is to make fun of Uncle Elisha, but he can't laugh this thing out of court."

This is what Mr. Lockhart said as introductory to his speech. Such an eloquent, profound exposition of law I never heard before. It indeed was a grand speech, embracing points of law and facts in every proposition and question. Sometime after this Mr. Gould was found guilty of immoral conduct and excluded from the church and conference of which he was a member.*

In conclusion let me say that I have no accurate account of the persons that I have baptized since I began preaching. When in Kansas two years ago the Rev. George W. Dupee said it must be in the neighborhood of 6,000. But whether it is this or less, I am conscious of the fact that my work has been blessed. God has never withheld from his humble servant any good thing. In all these years I cannot remember of closing a meeting without having gained some soul for Christ. Often and at times the way has looked dark and cloudy, but nevertheless, God came to my rescue. I would try to live so that I could tell my brethren and sisters "Follow me as I would follow Christ." I have always since my conversion, tried to follow Jesus Christ.

A word to the young ministers: A great responsibility now lies at your hands. God needs you to carry out his divine plan in the salvation of the world. We, the old veterans of the cross, are passing away. Soon we shall sleep with the fathers. Who will lead when we are gone? It rests with you to decide this important question. While this is an age of education and of progress in the sciences and arts, yet it is no less the age of immoral conduct. Possess your character and educate yourselves. You have no excuse now. If you go into the ministry uneducated in this day of enlightenment you show plainly you are not a progressive creature. Keep yourself pure from whisky, wine, beer or any other thing that degrades a man. It is my character that has kept me in Paris and Maysville for these thirty-odd years. You can do the same if you will live right, act right and do right. If I could call back forty-five years I would be seen grappling with language and the different sciences as other men. But slavery prevented me from getting an education. I came up in an age of unreconciliation between men—when books in a

_____
* I have the trial of the above statement.

black man's hand were equal to a case of murder sometimes in this day. But I thank God that that day has past and the glories of a better one are upon us. Young ministers, whatever you do, possess a good character. But have both character and education. Be men. and strong men. We old fathers have prepared the material for the building, and you must do the building. Do this and God will bless you.